CALLING ALL
MONSTERS

Chris Westwood

CALLING ALL
MONSTERS

HarperCollins*Publishers*

Quote on p. 1 from "The Wonderful Death of Dudley Stone" in *The October Country* by Ray Bradbury, reprinted by permission of Don Congdon Associates, Inc., and Abner Stein. Copyright © 1954; renewed 1982 by Ray Bradbury

Library of Congress Cataloging-in-Publication Data
Westwood, Chris.
  Calling all monsters / Chris Westwood.
    p.   cm.
  Summary: Having immersed herself in the books of horror writer Martin Wisemann, Joanne is shocked when the hideous monsters in the pages come to life and begin haunting her days and nights.
  ISBN 0-06-022461-4. — ISBN 0-06-022462-2 (lib. bdg.)
  [1. Horror stories.]   I. Title.
PZ7.W5274Cal   1993   91-19601
[Fic]—dc20   CIP
                                                            AC

For Anne and Alan,
and Stephen and Jade Leigh Blower—
may all your monsters be small ones

"Pass the hat," I said. "I'll travel three hundred miles, grab Dudley Stone by the pants and say: 'Look here, Mr. Stone, why did you let us down so badly? Why haven't you written a book in twenty-five years?'"

Ray Bradbury,
"The Wonderful Death of Dudley Stone" in
The October Country

1

IT WAS COMING UP FOR AIR.

Slowly, in the cool and the dark of its lair, it began to move. Beneath its body, which the cold had numbed of feeling, there was nothing: a thousand miles and more of solemn night; a silence never broken. But above—now there was something, a suggestion of scents and sounds and food, perhaps. Straining, it pushed its limbs forward and up. As it did so, its whole body seethed with pain. In what remained of its mind, it could find no recollection of its former shape.

Now relaxing, it tried hard to hold its thoughts. It had no idea how long it had lain here, or who had placed it in such an awkward position, or why. Surely there was more to life, if this was life, than blind endless dark and the feeling of suffocation.

Again, bracing itself, it tried to stand.

This time, something gave. Into its mouth came the taste of soil, to its fingertips the sensation of soft earth parting to make way. Life moved minutely through its touch. Here were worms, there grubs. Instinctively it could name these squirming creatures, remember their shapes. Perhaps its loss of memory had been sluggishness on waking. Encouraged, it pushed harder. Nearer the surface, the earth became drier and parted more easily.

The river of dark was receding. The surface was inches away. Its clawed hand found the air, clutched at turf, tore a handful up by the roots. Its lungs drew in deep, earthy breaths, the taste of dead leaves and wood bark. One more effort: a final lunge, a swimmer touching poolside. Sudden panic made it gasp aloud, but there was no turning back. There was a spotlight, overhead, trained on the very site it was emerging from. It was the moon, whole and pale above a cloudless night. The light it had dreamed of reaching, no longer a memory but tangible, real.

With a final flourish it dragged itself into the world. For a while it lay silently absorbing the light, collecting its senses. Standing as comfortably as its misshapen mass would allow, it looked around. This new environment seemed somehow familiar. Everywhere, slabs of stone or marble were set at sharp angles and tipped with moonlight like frost. Pale crosses stood at the feet of the stooping, blackened trees, and beyond the trees were the numberless jagged tips of an iron fence and a gate that was chained and padlocked. What was the idea—to keep intruders out or residents in?

It began moving again, toward the trees and the spike-topped railings. Beyond was a road, and a row of houses glowing warmly in a cast of streetlamps. Its movements were confused and awkward now that it was out of the ground; it couldn't quite synchronize its many limbs. But the angry sensation in its belly was familiar. It was hunger, and it hadn't forgotten how to hunt.

It had crossed the cool grass and nearly reached the locked gates when a sudden movement to the left caught its attention. Above, in the thickness of one of the trees, something fluttered and then fell silent. Without hesitation it scurried, quick as it could, to the foot of the tree. From the midst of the leaves it sensed the forced silence, the bated breath. The world spun silently, endlessly on until there was only the rustle of leaf upon leaf. As a light came on in a house across the street, the creature began the climb.

2

JOANNE WAS AWAKENED by the force of her own struggle. The first thing she was aware of was that something held her legs and cupped her mouth, restricting her breathing. Darkness covered everything. After a moment her tossing and turning ceased, and she lay perfectly still. Freeing one hand, she fumbled blindly for the bedside lamp and turned it on.

Suddenly everything made sense again. She lay facedown, nose and mouth buried in her pillow, legs coiled in the matted bedsheets. Had she been dreaming? Certainly she'd been perspiring. It was as if she'd been buried alive. Perhaps the book of horror stories on her night table, Martin Wisemann's *Dark Tales*, had been putting ideas in her head, but as yet she couldn't be sure what she'd dreamed. Beside the book was her half-empty glass of water. Straining against the sheets, she leaned across and took a sip.

With the faint taste of fluoride came hard reality. She was alone in her room, the shelves lined with favorite books, a shabby *Alien* poster pinned on the wall opposite. Go to work on an egg. In space no one can hear you scream. Her mind was still racing, unsettled. Convinced that nothing had changed, that the world was much as it always had been, she set to work freeing her feet from the tangled sheets. As she did so she heard the cry.

In fact what she heard was a mournful, trembling caterwaul, like that of a stray cat or a dog locked out for the night and forgotten. Perhaps that was all it was; but she hated the idea that something might be needlessly suffering out there. The things that people did to defenseless animals these days . . . But you couldn't take all the troubles of the world on your shoulders. No one could bear such burdens. Trying to forget what she'd heard, she turned back to the lamp at the bedside and turned it off.

No sooner had the room collapsed to dark—her finger was still on the switch—than the scream rose again. This time her body grew rigid. God, something would have to be suffering to produce such sounds as those. As long as she remained awake, she would have to do something. She'd never be able to rest if she didn't find out. Leaving the light off, she slid out of bed and crossed to the window for a view of the street.

When she'd wiped the mist from the pane, she could see more clearly. Peterborough Lane was asleep; the only cars within sight were parked, and there was no sign of movement in either the street or any of the small square front gardens. Nothing stirred in the amber glow of the streetlights. Far away, the town clock chimed twice. Margaret, her eldest sister, who had recently married and moved in four doors down, kept several cats, which she put out last thing at night; and occasionally Joanne had woken to their chorus, or the crash of a garbage can lid, cursing them quietly before returning to sleep. Couldn't that be what she'd just heard—the familiar howl of cats? The book she'd been reading and her restless sleep had made her imagine the rest.

But there was movement out there. Joanne had half turned from the window before she registered the commotion across the street, somewhere inside the cemetery gates. She leaned close to the window, squinting, gripping the sash. Unless she was much mistaken, something was shaking the lower branches of one of the trees, just to the right of the main path that bisected the burial grounds. She'd scarcely had time to establish the source of the movement when something flew out of the tree—an owl, perhaps, or a crow. Whichever, she saw only its silhouette, and en only briefly, for another shape was scuttling down from the branches.

As soon as she caught sight of the second creature, her breath gave out. Her nails, clutching the sash, dug into the woodwork. There must be something wrong with her vision, since what she was seeing had twice as many arms and heads as it ought to have. Surely the doubling effect was caused by shadow—the creature and its shadow self. But there wasn't enough time to be certain. Whatever the shape was, it was hurrying, nimbling to the ground, propelling itself toward the cover of headstones. Then it was swallowed by the dark.

Joanne stood there, shivering, wishing she'd thrown something on over her nightgown. In a distant street, somewhere beyond the cemetery, a dog broke into a howl. It couldn't be confused with the cry she'd heard, and it quickly fell silent. By the time Joanne had stared fully five minutes into the still beyond the street, she couldn't be sure she'd seen anything at all.

3

SHE VAGUELY REMEMBERED A VOICE calling her name from some remote other world—the foot of the stairs—but there was no knowing how long ago that had been. Then, with the blinding suddenness of a fine idea, it came to her. Sunlight blurred the face of her clock at the bedside, and she knew she must be late.

There was time, just, to wash, dress, seize a slice of cold buttered toast on the way to the bus. She was still tugging a sweatshirt over her head as she stumbled downstairs, and had almost reached the bottom before she realized someone was watching her.

It took her several more seconds, the rest of the way down, to confirm her first impression: The man was a uniformed cop. He was standing just outside the open front door and talking in hushed tones to her stepfather, David, who was folding his arms and tapping his foot as if to show that he too was late. Maybe the cop hadn't stared at her dressing, but he'd made her feel vulnerable, catching her so soon in the day. She looked determinedly away from him as she passed through the hall and into the kitchen.

"Something wrong?" she asked, flopping down at the table her mother was clearing. A mess of crumbs and congealed Rice Krispies told Joanne that Sarah had already passed this way and left for school.

Her mother pushed a steaming cup of tea toward Joanne and said, "They're speaking so quietly, I can't really hear. We'll know in a minute, probably. Can I get you something to eat with that?"

"No time," Joanne said. Besides which, she'd lost the small appetite she'd woken with. Her head felt both congested and empty, if that were possible. The need to hurry to school wasn't helping, nor was the kitchen clock's message. Her bus would have gone by now.

"We were calling you half an hour ago," her mother was saying. "Were you up late reading again?"

"Yes, but not as late as you'd think. I didn't—" Her thoughts were still muddled by impressions of dreams. "I didn't sleep too well. The nights are so warm just lately."

"All the same, you should at least try."

"You think I don't?"

11

"The staff at your school will think I'm responsible; they'll think I don't care." Shaking her head, her mother reached for the first morning cigarette and pulled up a chair opposite Joanne. As the cigarette was lit, Joanne balked; it felt like the onset of a lecture, the threat of headache.

But her mother said nothing at first. Watching Joanne with those ever-gentle gray eyes, she smoked and gradually smiled. Finally she lowered her gaze as though ashamed or embarrassed. "Who've you got first?"

"Geoff Curtis for Art. He's okay, don't worry."

"Should I write you a note?"

"I hope I'm past the stage where I need notes," Joanne said, and stood. "All the same, I'd better be going."

As she crossed to the sink with her untouched tea, she heard the front door slam. Though her view from the window was partly obscured by a flourish of privet hedges, she saw the uniformed cop closing the gate and crossing the street to the cemetery. The gates were now open. Two police vehicles were pulled up outside.

As David entered the kitchen behind her, Joanne wondered dreamily, "Isn't it darker in here than it should be, with all those hedges out front?"

"What did they want, then?" her mother asked.

"They wanted to know if we'd seen anything,"

David replied. "Someone vandalized the cemetery last night. Cracked the headstones, dug up soil."

"That's really scummy," Joanne said, pouring the contents of her cup away. "That's really about as low as you can get. What kind of person—?" she was about to finish, and then remembered the many-armed shape she had glimpsed in the tree. Of course, she'd seen nothing of the kind! Daylight lent a fresh complexion to everything, swept madness and doubt into corners like cobwebs.

"Whoever it was, you can't call them human," her mother said then and, coughing, put out her cigarette, which she'd barely touched. "God, I've got to give it up," she murmured. She had started again after Jason was born, almost two years ago. Joanne wondered whether having another child so late had been both a blessing and a curse to her mother. No one would have traded Jason for the world, but sometimes the strain was terribly noticeable.

"Where do you think you're going?" David called as Joanne reached the doorway. It was only as she turned, preparing herself for a confrontation, that she realized he wasn't dressed for work. "Come on, I'll give you a lift," he told her. "I've got the day off."

David drove her calmly through the South Horton streets with the radio on, only accelerating to outfox a traffic light changing from green to amber. She still hadn't found herself able to call him Father or Dad, even after three long years, but perhaps he didn't expect it from her. Only Sarah had managed to call him that without flinching.

For one thing, he was several years younger than Mother and barely eight or ten years older than Maggie. To Joanne he had always seemed, and still did seem, more like an older brother than anything. But not one to confide in or joke with; merely another presence, the man of the house. Some evenings after work, he arrived home smelling of beer.

He drove, this morning, with the sleeves of his checked shirt rolled up from his forearms, which were strong and tanned and brushed with dark hair like an ape's. Briefly, Joanne pictured him driving a forklift or Mack truck, though he worked in a specialist stereo shop—Audiodrome—downtown.

They were nearing the school on Loughborough Road before anyone spoke. David turned the radio down, and at first Joanne was only aware of the silence. Then he said, "So. This is your last day then."

"My last day?"

"Friday, remember. It's mid-term or something, isn't it? You've got a week's grace."

"Oh, yes." Joanne nodded vigorously. "I'd forgotten in all the rush. Yes, that's right."

"What will you do with yourself? Go swimming, dancing, partying all night long?" When Joanne laughed and shook her head, he added, "No, I suppose

14

not. Knowing you, you'll probably spend your week in the library. Or closeting yourself in your room."

"I'm not as bad as all that, David."

"Of course not."

"If you really want to know, I have an English assignment—a major project. If I have to closet myself, it won't be without good reason. And I'll be seeing Georgia, as usual."

"Hmmm." The conversation already seemed to be wearing thin, but the school was in sight, and he was dropping gears and signaling to pull up to the curb. "And you'll be seeing that boy of yours too, I suppose. That Billy McGuire. Isn't that his name?"

"That's right," she said, wishing he'd let the topic lie. It was like a stirring of silt in clear water. Just lately the mere mention of Billy made her grow tense, slowed down her thoughts until she felt incapable of dealing with anything. She had been meaning to call him since Monday and putting it off, finding reasons not to. "You can pull over here," she told David.

From the main street the school looked deserted, but that was because all the classes were in session. Thank goodness Geoff Curtis didn't worry about punctuality; usually he'd be too stoned to notice or care anyway. As she slipped from the car, David said, "Have a nice day," and sounded as though he meant it.

"I'll try," she said. Then, as an afterthought, "Were

15

we just making conversation, David, or are you seriously interested in what I do?"

"I'm seriously interested," he replied, smiling.

Slamming the door after her, adjusting her bag on her shoulder, she turned away toward school, wishing she could believe it. Perhaps she'd misjudged him; she'd like to believe so, but she could barely remember the last time they'd talked. Crossing the staff parking lot toward the art block, she couldn't help wondering what David would do with *his* day. She hoped he would spend it trimming the overgrown hedge in front of the house: That might keep the darkness outside, where it belonged.

4

SHE WAS STILL WONDERING how she might deal with Billy McGuire when she caught sight of him, making his way toward her across the open-air courtyard that was busy with drinkers. She ought to have known she wouldn't be able to hide for long.

Since seven in the evening, a calm summer's evening, she had been sitting with Georgia and Georgia's latest beau, Tim Lockwood, at a table in the beer garden behind Malone's wine bar. The manager, an old hippie liberal with a Legalize Pot button affixed to one lapel, had never asked for ID in all the time they'd been coming here.

For almost an hour they had talked warmly and easily about nothing in particular, enjoying the weather and the company. Now, too late, Joanne realized she should have asked Georgia's advice about Billy—there'd been plenty of time—but here he was, and her chance had gone. She suddenly felt as though the drinks had thickened her head, but she'd touched only mineral water.

"Hello, Jo," Billy said, levering himself in beside her on the narrow bench that was bolted to both table and ground. "You didn't say you were coming here."

"Didn't I?"

"If I didn't know better, I'd guess you'd been avoiding me," he said, and she felt herself flushing. "Who's this?" he asked brusquely.

Tim seemed visibly to flinch as Billy jabbed a thumb in his direction. He was fair haired and blue eyed, nervous and always quick to smile, and Joanne had liked him as long as she'd known him, not long in fact. When she'd first heard he was seeing Georgia, she hadn't been able to prevent a sudden, fleeting pang of jealousy; but he was so much better than the jerks Georgia had been with before, and Georgia deserved better.

"My name," Tim was about to volunteer, but Billy McGuire had already turned away. Finished drinking, Georgia put down her wineglass and began gnawing her lower lip.

"So what were you planning?" Billy said. "For the rest of the night, I mean. Or aren't I included?"

Oh God, here we go, Joanne thought. Already she sensed the evening falling apart. She might as well bring him along; in any case, she'd have to break the news sooner or later, and this might be her best opportunity. "The movies," she said. "We were going to see a film, weren't we, folks?"

"Which one?" Billy said, as if testing her.

"The Tom Cruise," Tim ventured. "A love story."

"Oh." Billy gazed thoughtfully at Tim, then at Georgia, and snickered. "I see. A love story."

"You don't have to come if you don't want," Georgia said rapidly. "If you'd prefer to see Rambo busting heads, there's always another screen."

"Well, I think I'll tag along, if it's all the same to you." Billy picked up Joanne's drink, took one sip, and made a face as he set it down. "Just to see what I might've been missing."

Why did he have to make everything sound like a threat or an accusation? Joanne wriggled free of the bench and stood rubbing her hands, though it wasn't cold. She mustn't speak her mind yet, not here and now; she wouldn't let Billy spoil the rest of the evening. As he stood to join her, his leather jacket creaking and his jaw moving circles around the wad of gum he always seemed to be chewing, she wondered what she had ever seen in him. An aching sadness passed through her and was gone. Right now he reminded her of an extra from a movie of an S. E. Hinton story; and that was his problem—he was acting the part, pretending to be something he wasn't.

"So." Joanne took a deep breath and smiled meekly at Georgia. "Is it all right for Billy to join us?"

"Of course it is. There's no need to ask me," Georgia said. To Billy she added, "You can do whatever you want."

She had always been good at diplomacy.

Billy had never been good at it, though. As soon as the lights were dimmed and the trailers began, Joanne wished she had sent him home instead. What was it about the dark that loosened inhibitions or increased them—made people bolder, brought their fears to the surface? Certainly, Billy seemed quickly transformed by it. The rating statement had scarcely faded from view when she felt an unwanted hand curling beneath her armpit to her breast.

It wouldn't have been so bad if he'd wanted her for anything else. When was the last time he had asked her about her studies, or which book she was reading? "Do you mind?" she hissed through the dark, and recoiled. In an instant she had forced his hand away and zippered her jacket to the throat, folding her arms across her chest. She heard him push air through his teeth in frustrated annoyance as an amorphous blob of gray matter appeared on the screen.

It was the trailer for *Revenge of the Slime*, the first of the multiplex theater's late-night horror previews. Suddenly she wished she were sitting through that instead; at the moment, with Billy beside her, the subject matter seemed more appropriate than that of a love story. Now the blob had found its way into a house, through the bathroom taps. An anemic young man, caught in the middle of shaving, dropped his razor and screamed. The blob was surging toward him, filling the bathroom with grayness, when the trailer cut to a frame of credits, then blackness. "You'll never shave alone again!" someone called drunkenly from the back. In the silence before the next trailer, Joanne was acutely aware of Billy, seething beside her, sinking lower into his seat.

"I don't know what's wrong with you," he said, a little too loudly for her liking. One or two featureless gray heads in front of them turned to stare.

She leaned toward him, not too close. "I think we need to talk, Billy. Later."

"About what?"

"I'll explain everything later."

"You're making no sense. Why did you want me along if all you were going to do was ignore me?"

Someone behind them was making a shushing noise. Potato chip packs rattled in every anonymous row. Joanne turned back to the screen. A limping murderer was stalking the blue-lighted streets of his hometown, knife in hand. She knew this one, she was certain; it was based on a novel she'd read. She remembered the girl screaming for help in the kitchen, rooting through cupboards for anything to defend herself with. She remembered the cellar door slamming shut.

To her right, Joanne heard the hushed whispered conversation between Georgia and Tim. When had she last been able to speak to Billy so intimately? Indeed, had she ever? She turned away as they kissed. To her left, all she heard was the smacking of Billy's lips as he chewed. No wonder she was depressed by the time the trailers gave out and the feature began.

The film itself only made her feel worse. Everything in the story seemed like a reference to Billy and her. Did the scriptwriters know all her secrets? Of course, Billy could never pass for Tom Cruise, not even in the movies with the lights down; but everything else was there. The film was simply unbelievable. The characters, Cruise and a girl Joanne couldn't place, never really connected. They courted, kissed, and squabbled, and never at any time had anything in common. While the girl poured her heart out to friends and family, Cruise was out seeing other girls; different girls every night, models all. How could they keep going as long as they had without really liking one another? Couldn't the girl see what a creep she'd landed?

Finally it seemed that something would give. Joanne sat forward, her interest growing. The girl was in tears, but tears of righteous anger at last: She'd discovered what Cruise had been doing those nights when he'd claimed to be working late. Her parents had never approved of him. They were urging her to pick up the telephone. Now, as she tried for the first time to reach a decision, someone was blocking Joanne's vision.

It was Billy who stood before her, his bulk almost filling the screen. "Come on," he said, leaning near. His voice was kept low, but she could sense the anger that would soon make him shout. "We've had enough of this; we're leaving."

Joanne held her ground. "You might've had enough, but *we're* staying."

"You don't understand," Billy said. Ignoring the calls to sit down and be quiet, he took hold of Joanne by both wrists. In the darkness, her senses seemed heightened; she could smell gum on his breath and the tang of stale sweat on his clothing. "You've been avoiding me long enough," he was saying. "If you've something to tell me, you'd better tell me now."

"Let *go* of me!" Joanne protested, barely controlling her volume. Sooner or later her anger would burst; she'd surely explode. More voices were raised. There was scuffling as Tim stood up to help and was pushed firmly back in his seat. As Billy tugged her along the cramped row, a harsh brightness flashed into Joanne's eyes. Squinting, she raised a hand to block the light.

"Joanne?" Georgia said.

"It's all right," Joanne said quickly. "You stay here—I can handle this."

"You'd better try handling it outside, then," a voice said. It was the man who wielded the flashlight.

"That's just what we're doing," Billy replied, leading the way.

"After the film," Joanne said over her shoulder to Georgia. "I'll wait for you outside. Don't worry."

Billy McGuire was still clutching her wrist as they marched through the foyer of the multiplex. Where did he think she would run to? She was so incensed that she couldn't speak; she might have told him what she thought of him if she hadn't been so utterly embarrassed. Instead, gritting her teeth, she glared at the monster posters promoting the theater's midnight horror shows as if wishing they would come alive.

The cinema and its five screens were on the second level of a shoppers' paradise—the Arcadia Center, whose mirrored walls, fountains, and trees planted into the concrete floors had always seemed to Joanne a designer's bad dream. Just now, so late, her footsteps sounded painfully loud in the empty vastness of it all. Only the escalators stirred on the building's three levels. As she and Billy started down, she watched hanging baskets of exotic flowers and shop-window mannequins wearing the latest fashions slide above her, out of sight. Now and again she caught herself in a mirror, anxious eyed. Then she was on the ground level and facing one of the exits, the one that let directly onto the main street.

"Will you let go of me now?" she said as he pulled her out through the doors toward the traffic. "That hurts; you're blocking my circulation."

Billy released her wrist. His fingerprints lingered there, pink and white. Darkness had fallen while they'd been inside, and Joanne was relieved to find all the town's lights glowing brightly. It was as though she and Billy stood on a stage: He wouldn't dare try hurting her now, or someone would see.

"Well," he said. "Here we are, then."

"Yes. Here we are."

"Ruined your evening, have I?"

"You haven't exactly been the life and soul of the party."

"That's typical of you: never able to see faults in yourself, only in other people."

Joanne could only laugh, though she felt like screaming, lashing out with her fists to beat the sense back into him.

Billy's eyes seemed to blaze as he said, "Well? You've something to say to me. It sounded pretty important before. Better get it off your chest, hadn't you?"

Joanne could not meet his eyes. The words were deserting her. It was now or never, but wasn't he making it easy for her, behaving this way? She stood, hands pocketed, while he waited. Across the street, at the mouth of the pedestrian mall, the

Doncaster bus pulled into its stop, collected two passengers, moved on.

"Billy," she said, "I've been trying to get around to this all week, really I have. If it seems I've been avoiding you, I'm sorry. I'd been meaning to call, and putting it off because I couldn't be sure how you'd take it. You see—" It was working; the words were coming after all; all she had needed to do was take the initial plunge. And Billy was listening. His doubting, frowning expression wasn't distracting her at all, as she'd feared it might. She was about to go on when he turned sharply away. Behind him, a car horn blared, and brakes shrieked.

Joanne looked up, astonished. How could this happen now, just when she'd conjured up everything she needed to say? But now she'd lost it: As soon as she saw what was happening on the street, words failed her. A pale stooping figure, no larger than a child, had darted out in front of a Ford Capri. Its movements were low and astonishingly quick. In the split second it took to pass through the headlights, Joanne saw it clearly.

Everything else happened, it seemed, in slow motion. The driver of the Ford swerved to miss. No one stood at the bus stop, a red-and-white sign attached to a lamppost. The figure flitted past and was gone, toward the safety of the pedestrian mall. As Joanne lost sight of it, she heard the impact of the car against the post.

"My God," Billy said, already running. "You see that?"

Without thinking, she followed him into the street. A crowd was gathering at the foot of the post, which had kinked back acutely from the road where the vehicle had stalled.

"That stupid bloody kid," Joanne heard someone say. "What's the matter with these kids today anyway?" But what kid? Had her eyes deceived her again? Surely what she'd seen had been something not exactly human.

"What happened?" another of the sightseers wondered now.

A man wearing thick-lensed glasses like the bases of jam jars explained, "A dog, I think it was. Someone should have had it on a leash. There ought to be a law or something."

"There is," another said.

Pedestrians were tugging at both doors of the Ford at once. The driver lay slumped forward over the steering wheel. A halo of broken windshield glass crowned his head. But at least he was moving, and when a policeman arrived to begin taking over, Joanne started to walk away.

It was then that she noticed the face in the crowd. Suddenly she was looking directly into the eyes of a man, probably in his early or middle forties, who was backing slowly away from the scene. She noticed small details before she realized it—the slight wisps of gray at his temples, the weatherbeaten look of the single-breasted suede jacket he wore. A look passed between them, like a glance between acquaintances who had known one another for years, and she had never seen such fear in a face in her life. It was over in an instant. The man turned and walked quickly away, toward the town library near the edge of the mall.

Then Joanne heard a shout, her name being called above the traffic noise. It wasn't Billy, who was staring fascinated at the accident. Across the street, Georgia and Tim were standing in front of the Arcadia Center. They were either the first out or had left the film early, concerned about Joanne. She waved feebly, not really aware she was doing so. She couldn't get the man's face out of her mind. The look in his eyes. It was as though, on seeing the crash, he'd been overtaken by a single terrible thought; as though he had realized that he was to blame.

5

FOR ONCE SHE WAS ABLE TO FEEL GRATEFUL for the potholes on the local roads. The bus jerked sharply, and she woke from half sleep to find herself alone on the upper deck.

Fortunately she hadn't overslept her stop, though she almost had. The bus was making the familiar sweeping left turn onto Fairview Road, which intersected the foot of Peterborough Lane. Thumbing the bell push, Joanne tumbled down the spiral staircase and out through the hissing doors.

Really, she ought to be feeling bright as day. A crescent moon tipped the slanting rooftops, keeping pace with her as she walked. The mild night air felt invigorating as rain on her skin. She ought to be facing the forthcoming week with pleasure, not brooding over the evening's disasters—the car accident on the main street, her failure to tell Billy the truth. She needed to catch up on the sleep she'd missed last night, that was all. But shouldn't she call Billy first, get it over with? Hurrying now, she turned left onto the home stretch, past the cemetery.

The branches of trees groped over the railings as she passed. Between the uprights she could see several pale shapes, keeping as still as possible, deep in the heart of the cemetery. They were gravestones though, trapped by patches of moonlight. She should be used to the patterns of light and shade in there by now. Even so, quickening her step, she crossed to the other side of the street.

The house lights were on at home, and there were sounds of TV gun battles in the hall. Sarah and Jason would be asleep. When she'd hung up her coat, she poked her nose in the living room. David lay fast asleep in an armchair in front of the TV, where a western was playing. Curled on the sofa in front of the fire, her mother was lost in a James Clavell novel the thickness of a loaf. For one disconcerting moment Joanne felt like a visitor. She cleared her throat, and her mother looked up.

"Oh, hello. Aren't you early? Did you have a good time?"

Joanne waved a hand. "So-so. Is it all right if I use the phone?"

"Course you can, go ahead." Joanne was retreating from the room when her mother added, "Oh, I forgot to mention, you'd better not stay on too long. There may be a call from your uncle Ted in the Midlands; Mary fell ill tonight. Apparently they had to rush her to the hospital."

"What's wrong?"

"They think it's a stroke. By the sounds of it, she'll be lucky if she makes it through tonight."

"Good God." Wasn't life just a bowl of bitter cherries? In the armchair, David snored in the depths of sleep. "All right, I'll be quick," Joanne said, "and to the point."

The telephone rested on a low glass shelf just outside the living room door. Above it was an oval mirror, in which Joanne could watch herself dialing. Her face seemed to tighten as the call went through—she wanted to hang up right away. While she waited for someone to answer, something shifted and creaked in the dark midway along the hall, between the stairs and the kitchen door. From here she couldn't determine what, but it didn't matter, nothing mattered, because Billy McGuire was saying, "Hello?"

"It's Joanne," she said, breathing out.

"Really?" Even now, his voice sounded tinged with suspicion.

"I didn't know whether you'd be home yet."

"Well. Here I am. I'm amazed you remembered the number, it's so long since you called."

"Let's not start that again, Billy."

There was silence on the line for a second. Then he

said, "I missed you after the accident. You didn't waste much time getting away, did you?"

"I had to take a bus with Georgia."

"Sure you did. And that sidekick she was with, that creep."

"He does have a name. His name is Tim."

"So what's that got to do with me? And what are you calling for? Just to say hi?"

"To say good-bye, Billy."

There: It was finally out. A further extended silence told her she'd reached him at last, she'd taken him unawares.

Just when she thought Billy must have hung up, he said, "What do you mean by that?"

"I mean that it's over—you and me. I think we should stop seeing each other."

"Why?" he said. "Why? I don't understand. Why are you doing this to me?"

Good grief, he couldn't be as stupid as that. He sounded like a child on the verge of tears, whining and babbling. Surely he knew they had been coming to this. In recent weeks they'd scarcely been able to communicate at all without bickering. Didn't that mean anything to him?

But it was over now; she had managed to say it. She finished quickly, "That's all there is to it, Billy. I'm sorry, but I know it's for the best, for both of us. We can still be friends, can't we?"

He was laughing now. Or was he crying? She was

clutching the receiver tightly, and was so transfixed she was hardly aware of the soft thump somewhere along the hall. "I have to hang up now, Billy. I don't think there's anything more to say."

"I loved you, though." He was pleading as though he hadn't heard. "Didn't you know how much I cared? Joanne, let's talk about this reasonably—"

Gently she replaced the receiver, cutting him off. For a matter of seconds she stood over the phone, holding herself to calm her nerves. She was physically shaking. Weren't you supposed to feel relief at times like this? Probably she would feel that later. Now all she wanted was to crawl into bed, claw back the sleep she owed herself, and please make it dreamless!

Before she reached the stairs, she heard it again, the faintest of movements in the dark between the stairs and the kitchen. It was only the door to the basement, which David had forgotten to close and which a draft was moving. Within the past year, he had turned what had once been a grubby and disused coal cellar into a stereo workshop and listening room with carpets, bean bags, the works. She tugged the door shut and had turned back to the stairs when the phone began warbling.

Her first thought was that it must be bad news about Mary. She caught up the receiver, still warm from use.

"You don't know what you've done," a voice told

her. She recognized it almost at once as Billy's. "I can tell you this, I'm not going to let you get away with it. You may think I'm not good enough for you, but I am: I'll show you how special I am."

"Billy, are you threatening me? Because if you are—"

But this time it was Billy who hung up. She heard the faint click and the silence, and then the return of the dial tone, and again she replaced the receiver. Almost at once the phone began purring. She snatched it up quickly, not thinking. Her voice sounded cracked with anger. "Yes, what is it now?"

It was Uncle Ted with news of Mary. Her mother stood in the living room doorway, still holding her book, a forefinger marking her place. "Just a minute," Joanne told the mouthpiece and, handing it over, marched upstairs.

She didn't want to hear the outcome of the telephone call. She sensed instinctively it wouldn't be good. What she needed was sleep, and perhaps first a good long soak in the tub, drain away the day's frustrations. Before she reached the bathroom, she stopped to look in on Sarah and Jason. The sight of the two of them fast asleep—Sarah lost in a heap of bedsheets, Jason behind the bars of his crib—heartened her, and she suddenly wanted to run in and hug them both. Instead she entered quietly and crossed to the curtains. A broad gash of moonlight lay across Jason's chest and throat. If he turned directly into it, he would wake. His sleeping figure vanished into blackness as she pulled the curtains together.

While she waited for the bath to finish running, Joanne went through her collection of books. Many of these were horror and ghost stories; some she'd bought from market stands and secondhand shops and hadn't managed to read yet. She still had to find a topic for her English project, and had only a week to produce it. Would Miss Rees accept a treatise on werewolves and banshees? Perhaps not, but surely it made sense to choose something you knew about.

She had one more story from *Dark Tales* to go, and then she would have to begin something else. Maybe another of Martin Wisemann's, either *Death Toll* or *Desolation Day*; she had always liked his sense of the outrageous, and could lose herself quickly and fully in anything he wrote. Was he still writing? she wondered. It seemed such a long time since his last publication. Then she remembered a story she'd read, in one of his early collections. Hadn't he written the one about the thing being born in the graveyard, hauling itself up into the world? The interesting point, she remembered, was the fact that the story was told from the creature's point of view. Everything that was normal had been made to seem monstrous. Wondering, she skimmed her fingers along the spines of the books.

Here it was: She had the collection in hardback, good as new. She took it over to the bed and sat down to scan the contents page, where the words *This book belongs to Joanne Towne* had been literally carved into the page in pencil. The handwriting was Sarah's. None of the titles in the book rang a bell, but she could always check through it later. She had no time now: From here her bath sounded dangerously full.

She dropped the book on the bed and stood up. As she did, she noticed the author photograph on the back of the dust jacket and promptly sat down again. So this was Martin Wisemann. Why hadn't she noticed this shot of him before, when she'd first read the book? Of course she'd seen it before, but had quickly forgotten, since the man in the photograph could have been anyone; in every way he looked unremarkable. The kind of face you might miss in a crowd. Unless, she realized with a shudder, you happened to have seen him in the crowd on the main street tonight, backing away from the scene of the crash with fear in his eyes.

6

IT WAS HER SATURDAY ROUTINE to meet Georgia for lunch in Middleton and to browse through the clothing and book shops for hours, often without buying anything. Now and then they might take in an afternoon show at the multiplex. Unless she was flush with money—hardly ever—they would rendezvous in Arcadia, at one of the cheap fast-food stands on the ground floor near to where the fountains were surrounded with plastic palm trees and formica tables. They would wait for two chairs to empty and sit for an hour, discussing—bitching about, Georgia would call it—the people they knew, what they were doing, and with whom. It was the one day of the week Joanne looked forward to; her one chance to step out of herself and let go. Sometimes she wished she were more like Georgia:

sociable, able to fit any scene. But then she'd be missing other things. Georgia knew how to go out and tackle the real world head-on, but she hadn't read for pleasure in years.

The start of the weekend, then, and Joanne forced herself up out of bed, undressed in the bathroom, washed, dressed, and came clambering over the baby gate at the foot of the stairs. Jason was already up and about, picking things up, throwing things down, opening cabinets and drawers. He squealed with pleasure while her mother pursued him from room to room, gasping for breath, laughing in spite of herself.

"Morning," Joanne said brightly, but perhaps her mother didn't hear. Having finally caught up with Jason, she was lifting him onto her shoulder to carry him to the living room.

Joanne entered the kitchen, which seemed darker than ever. Shadows clung to corners; a patch of darkness like rising damp had stolen the wall above the washing machine. Through the window she saw David, moving his clippers back and forth along the hedge, and not a moment too soon.

She sat at the breakfast table with apple juice, All-Bran, and coffee before her. She seemed to have slept her emotional aches away, thank goodness. This morning the thought of Billy McGuire hardly bothered her at all. But Martin Wisemann's face was still with her. Since when had he been in town? Might he be a resident here, or was he just passing through?

She must find out. She was wondering how she might locate him when Sarah came in, still wearing pajamas and yawning and stretching.

"Morning, brat," Joanne said.

Sarah scowled. She was past her ninth birthday now, but the scowl always made her look years younger. "Why are you always calling me that? It's a good thing you caught me on a good day, or I'd— I'd—"

"You'd what?"

Sarah poured apple juice into a mug, taking her time. "Are you going to town today, then? You're wearing makeup, aren't you? You always wear makeup when you go into town."

"I'm only wearing a little," Joanne said.

But Sarah went on, "You're wearing it for that boy, I'll bet. That boy you've been seeing. Really, I don't know why you bother. Mom doesn't like him, you know. *I* don't like him, either. I saw him outside my school once, and he wouldn't speak to me. He was with some other boys, and I'll bet he thought it was sissy, or something, to say hello. I don't know what the big deal is with boys. I think they're so stupid, most of them."

Joanne placed her cup in its saucer and smiled. "You're right, they are. As a matter of fact, I won't be seeing him anymore."

"Good," Sarah said, and that was the end of it. Joanne heard the hedge clippers snap together four, five times before Sarah said, "Do you ever have funny dreams?"

"Funny?"

"Well, not funny ha-ha, but *funny*."

"I'm not sure I know what you mean."

Sarah rolled her eyes heavenward. "You're hopeless, but I'll tell you anyway. I had this one last night, and you were in it. You came into my room while I was asleep—"

"How would you know I was there if you were asleep?"

"I was asleep in the dream is how. I dreamed you came into my room, and went to the curtains and shut them, and then you went out."

"That wasn't a dream—it really happened. I did come into your room."

But Sarah was shaking her head as though she knew better. "What I dreamed was, I dreamed there was something in the dark; a monster or something, waiting for its chance to come out. But it was all right, because the curtains were open, and there was just enough light to stop the monster from doing what it wanted to do. And I could see Jason sleeping in the light, and as long as the light was on him, he'd be safe. And then you came in and took the light away, and I could hear the monster getting ready to come out."

"And did it?"

"No, because then, in the dream, I woke up. Whatever it was, I could hear it breathing and licking its lips in the dark. So I ran to the curtains and pulled them open again, and the light came in."

"That's good," Joanne said, checking her Swatch. The bus that would take her into town was due in ten minutes. "And this thing that you heard, it left when you opened the curtains?"

"Yes. I saw it outside on the back lawn, staring up at my window for a minute before it ran away. At first I thought it might be a dog, but you could tell that's not what it was—it couldn't fool me. I never saw a dog that looked like that."

"Like what?"

But Sarah was suddenly lost in thought, gripping her chin like a philosopher. Outside there was the sound of a manual lawn mower, the distant throb of a motorbike. Then Sarah was staring intently into Joanne's eyes, laying her hand on Joanne's. "You wouldn't really do that to me, would you? Leave me in the dark so the monster could come? As long as there's light, you see, I'd be safe . . ." She trailed off, still worried.

Now, softening, Joanne took both her sister's hands in her own. "Of course I wouldn't let that happen. But you know what? If there were monsters out there, they'd probably have the guts to show themselves in light as well as the dark. And why don't they? Because they're imaginary, really they are, that's why. You've nothing to worry about, dummy."

"But if there *are* no monsters," Sarah said dubiously, "why do you read all those books that say there are?"

"They're made-up stories," Joanne tried to explain, "and I read them because—" Well, why *did* she? In any case, Sarah looked less than convinced. And besides, she'd run out of time; her bus was due in five minutes.

She sat near the back of the crowded lower deck of the 48 bus, watching Fairview Road slip away. The seats were taken by mothers and children, mostly, with their empty shopping bags ready to be filled. In front yards, husbands were cutting their lawns or hosing down their cars. Despite the smell of the bus, she could pick out the fragrance of fresh-cut grass, which for some reason raised her spirits.

It was a fact of life, though, that monsters existed, but it wasn't a fact she could admit to Sarah, not if she meant to reassure her. They came in many guises, but some she'd experienced firsthand. Her father had succumbed to a stroke when she was almost eleven, and had been dead on arrival at the hospital: That was the first she had known of true monsters, how swift they could be when they struck, how final their actions were. Some were like Billy

McGuire, not so much lethal as subtle, showing one face to begin with, then another quite different face later on. There were demons in disguise wherever you looked, tempting students to turn up drunk for exams, sending grown men to do away with themselves for want of work. Perhaps she should have told Sarah, I read about made-up monsters to learn how to deal with the real ones. Then she remembered Sarah's frown, her look of mistrust and disbelief. How could she expect her to swallow that?

But her thoughts were suffocating her. She needed to get her act together before she met Georgia or she'd ruin the day. She was wondering whether Tim would be there when the bus pulled up, jolting her forward in the seat.

It was the stop on Ashbourne Close, the one nearest Billy McGuire's house. Not so long ago, on those Saturday mornings when she and Billy had arranged to go into town together, this had been where he boarded. They had always taken a seat upstairs so that Billy could sprawl with one arm around her and smoke, and she'd tasted the smoke when he kissed her, and tasted it for hours after that. It was a habit she was only too pleased to be breaking.

Why were her memories of Billy such negative ones? It must have been good to begin with, or it would never have lasted. She'd forget him for good once she began her English assignment. Now she sat with her hands in her lap, lulled by the engine's shuddering. At the front of the bus, passengers were lining up to pay the driver. A fat woman nudged her shopping cart along the aisle, and as the line moved forward, Joanne shrank down in her seat when she saw that the last in the line was Billy.

He hadn't seen her, she was certain. For the moment she was obscured by a woman's hair, a straw-colored crow's nest humming with perm. If he looked this way, though, she was done for. She felt her heart speeding up. It didn't help that the fat woman seemed to have lodged her shopping cart against Joanne's seat as she passed, and had now begun cursing as if that would shift it. Please don't make a fuss, Joanne thought. You'll only draw attention. She still hadn't budged the cart when Joanne saw Billy McGuire go thundering upstairs.

The bus was already moving. Clutching her cart, the fat woman tumbled toward the back. When she was sure the threat had passed, Joanne squirmed upright in her seat again. A freckle-faced kid across the aisle stared as if there were something wrong with her.

She watched through the grimy window while landmarks came and went. A pub called The Three Horseshoes; a glimpse of the River Don beside the road. For several minutes there was countryside; the road swept rapidly downhill, a pedestrian footpath appearing and vanishing over a humpbacked bridge. She'd followed that beaten track once: It meandered through woodlands to emerge in Westbury, a quaint little grouping of three or four cottages set out like a toy village. She couldn't quite visualize it now—it was too long ago—but she still remembered her father pointing to one thatch-roofed building and saying, One day I'll have you a place like this to live in, just you wait. Well, she *had* waited, but the monsters had taken her father away before he could act.

Soon the outskirts of town were upon her again, and the bus was tackling the busy main traffic circle. It occurred to Joanne suddenly that she and Billy had always alighted near Arcadia, opposite the pedestrian mall. If she jumped off several stops before then, she might get away without being seen. She'd better get off before the main street.

She moved forward between the seats, hesitating at the foot of the stairs in case of anyone coming down. As the bus straightened up, she jabbed the bell several times, angrily. Why should she let Billy intimidate her? His phone call last night was an immature outburst—she'd tell him so when she saw him again.

She stepped from the platform almost before the bus had stopped moving. The bus windows had made the day appear overcast, but in truth it was marvelous; you could see the good weather in people's faces. The shirt sleeves were out and short skirts were in. Everyone's flesh seemed golden, if not brown, which made her feel paler than ever. Just before the bus moved away again, she chanced a glance

45

back at it. Billy was watching her from an upstairs window, his face so close to the glass, he was misting it over.

In fact the mist was because he was speaking—trying to tell her something. Judging by his expression, she was glad she couldn't hear what. Then suddenly he was no longer at the window, and she knew he must be heading downstairs. Joanne froze, unsure what to do next. She saw Billy appear at the doors too late, as the bus was pulling into traffic.

The next stop, outside Woolworth's, couldn't be more than two hundred yards away. Any second he'd be racing along the street toward her, the last thing she needed to deal with. She walked quickly in the opposite direction, waited for a gap in the stream of pedestrians, then slipped into Sutton Mews, a side street dominated by florists' windows and the smell of fresh bread.

Some of her favorite old shops were here—you could almost forget how the shopping mall had taken over. One window was dominated by antique rag dolls and mechanical clowns, another by standing and hanging brasses, light fittings, table lamps. Here was her favorite of all, The Egg Shop, so called because it stocked everything but eggs. In its display were old records, a wedding dress, and a snowstorm paperweight. Next door was the sign that said CARLETON'S BOOKSELLERS. She shuddered to think how many hours she'd whiled away here. Checking behind her—no sign of Billy—she stepped inside.

A bell clanked as the door was opened and closed. Although it was Saturday, the place was empty except for balding Mr. Carleton himself, who was seated behind the modern electronic cash register, poring over a trade magazine. He looked up as Joanne entered, smiled broadly without seeing her, and went on reading. Presumably the Bradbury novel she'd ordered hadn't arrived yet, or he would have said. But she had more important things on her mind now. She moved quickly through the cramped downstairs, past the paperback shelves labeled Horror, SF, Thrillers, to the flight of wooden steps and the upper floor, where the reference books were kept.

The advantage of the upstairs section, she knew, was that hardly anyone ever used it. The shelves here smelled aged and musty, and a decrepit mahogany table and chair were positioned near the single arch window where the light fell upon them, exposing their scratches. More than once in the past, Mr. Carleton had allowed Joanne to bring her schoolbooks and settle up here to study. The smell of ancient books always seemed to inspire her. Now she positioned herself by the window to watch out for Billy. From here she'd be able to see anyone turning into the mews from the main street.

Was she overreacting? Probably, but then she *had* seen the other face of Billy McGuire; the one that was there when the charm wore off. Again, there was last night's phone call. Whatever his stupid threats had meant, he'd certainly sounded serious. She drummed her fingers on the table and waited. Five minutes later, no one had approached from the street. She was relaxing back in the chair when she heard the bell downstairs.

The stairs descended to a open doorway, beyond which was the shop. From the top she couldn't see who had come in, but she could quickly tell that it wasn't Billy. There was a curt exchange of male voices—hello; good morning—followed by silence as the customer began to browse. Joanne went back to the window and waited a further five minutes before returning to the stairs. She doubted she'd see Billy again today.

Starting down, she heard the first of a series of electronic *bip*s, the sound of Mr. Carleton running his light pen over the bar-coded books he was selling. Eight or nine *bip*s had passed by the time she made it downstairs: The customer must be spending a fortune. She passed through the doorway in time to see a man in a blue windbreaker edging away from the counter, moving lopsidedly because of his shopping bag full of books. He hadn't taken long, but he'd obviously found what he'd wanted.

"Have you seen enough?" Mr. Carleton said cheerfully when he saw Joanne. The man with the shopping bag stopped at the door and turned, perhaps thinking Mr. Carleton had been speaking to him. The sight of him stopped Joanne in her tracks. It was Martin Wisemann; this time she did not have to look twice to be sure.

So she hadn't been mistaken—he really was here in the flesh. But what difference did that make to anything? What should she do, or say? She felt helpless as a puppet, watching him turn away again, the bell sounding rustily as he opened the door. In a second he'd be gone forever, and she'd have missed her only chance. She hadn't the least idea what to say, and her voice sounded cracked with nerves as she called after him, "Martin, isn't that you?"

7

AT FIRST HE SEEMED NOT TO HEAR. His back was turned as she spoke, and the door was already swinging shut. He stumbled away, weighed down by books. Joanne followed him out, and he had reached The Egg Shop's window display before she caught up, laying a hand on his arm, gasping as though out of breath.

"It really is," she said, "isn't it?"

"Isn't what?"

"Isn't it you?"

He appeared to relax at that, to study her with sudden interest and amusement. "Apparently it *is* me. Have we met before?"

"Not exactly. There was an accident not far from here last night; I saw you there. I thought you'd noticed me, but I couldn't be sure."

"Oh, *that.* Yes, I remember. There was a lot of confusion, everyone talking at once. I'm not one of those people who like to stand and stare."

"I noticed. You left very quickly."

He nodded and said, "To be truthful, I always *want* to stand and stare; I just don't like the idea of doing it." He stood for a moment with the shopping bag held in front of his chest, and at last his good humor passed. "I'm sorry. I didn't get your name."

"It's Joanne," she told him. "Joanne Towne."

"Ah, Joanne. Well, it's very good to meet you. But I'm not sure I understand what this is about. Did you have a reason for wanting to talk to me?"

Some impression she must be making: Nothing she'd told him so far had made sense. What on earth did she want to say? In the end she shrugged by way of apology. "I should have explained straight off—I knew your face from one of your books. I've read just about all of them—most of them, anyway. *Nightstalk* and *Forbidden Worlds* and *Into the Void.* And some of the story collections. I think you're the best."

"I'm flattered," he said, though he didn't seem especially so. "Listen, I'm in kind of a hurry. Do you mind if we walk? My car's just around the corner."

Were all authors as unsociable as this one? No wonder, if they spent most of their lives locked away from the world. She shouldn't judge him too quickly, she thought, but already she felt vaguely disappointed. His stories, after all, were so outlandish, so

51

alive with color. She was jogging to keep up as he turned right onto the main street, and had to shout above the traffic to make herself heard.

"Martin—Mr. Wisemann. I was wondering what you're doing these days."

"What I'm doing?"

"Whether you're writing another book. You see, I took half an hour to look through all your books last night. I noticed you hadn't had one published in more than ten years."

"Really?" He blew air through his lips appreciatively. "It's really as long as all that?"

"It really is. The last was your book of short stories *Cold Comforts*, I think, ten or eleven years ago. So have you given up writing now? I'm sorry if my questions are bothering you."

"No, your questions aren't bothering me, Joanne. Forgive me if that's the impression you get, but there really is something I have to do. Please don't think I'm brushing you off." He slowed as they rounded the corner into another side street where the cars were double-parked, and stopped beside a Volks- wagen Beetle whose tires were caked with mud. Unlocking the vehicle on the driver's side, he tossed his shopping bag onto the passenger seat and turned back to Joanne. "As a matter of fact I am still writ- ing. I just don't publish these days."

Joanne frowned. "Why not?"

"Let's just say it's because, now, I have a choice in

the matter, and I've chosen not to."

"Then why bother writing at all?"

"Ah, because that's a matter I have *no* choice in. It's something I have to do." When he saw the look on her face, he added, "Don't worry, you can't be expected to understand; it would take too much explaining."

In one fluid motion he jumped in behind the wheel, slammed the door, wound down the window. As he turned the ignition key, she realized what it was she had needed to say; the reason she'd approached him in the first place. "Mr. Wisemann," she said.

"Martin," he said.

"Would it be too much to ask if we could finish this conversation sometime? It may not mean much to you, but I've an English assignment and a week to do it in, and I think you might be able to help me out."

"How? Do you want me to write it?"

"No, but why couldn't I make you the subject? I know your work pretty well, and I could talk to you about everything you've done, and—" She was stopped by his doubting expression. "Maybe it's not such a great idea."

"Maybe not," he agreed flatly.

"All the same, will you at least think about it?" She could feel her hopes sliding; her fists were clenched at her sides. "Please?" she said desperately.

"I'll give it some thought," he said. "It's too soon

to make any definite promises." Briefly he fell silent and gazed into space, patting the wheel, as though privately trying to reach a decision. He revved up the engine several times before speaking again. "Listen, this is what we'll do. You're obviously serious about this; you seem to know my work. But how well *do* you know it?"

"Well enough, I suppose. How do you mean?"

"Did it ever do anything more than entertain you? Did it ever affect you in any deeper way?"

She faltered. "I don't know; I'm not sure I understand."

"Well, you should understand if you propose to go any further. If my stories are just entertainments to you, then I really can't help. Why don't you come to the house, and I'll try to explain. We'll talk everything through before you decide you still want to go on with your project."

Joanne nodded furiously. "Yes, that would be fine, perfect, thank you . . ."

"You'll find me about a mile and a half south of town. There's a track that leads away from the main road. You'll be able to get off the bus near there. Follow the path along the edge of the field until you come to a bridge—"

"Westbury," Joanne interrupted. "You're in Westbury, aren't you?"

"You know it?"

"I think of it every day. I used to dream of living there."

Martin nodded. "It is a dream home of sorts, I suppose. You'll find me there most hours of the day. Drop by when you can, and we'll see how things work out. Now"—he glanced at his watch and eased the VW into gear—"you'll have to excuse me."

"Yes, of course. Thank you," she said, but her words were lost as he pulled out from the curb and sped to the junction. She watched him turn left into the flow of traffic and stood for several seconds after he'd gone, her mind crowding with questions about him. At last she remembered Georgia. She set off, following the route the VW had taken, and by the time she was halfway to Arcadia, she was running.

8

GEORGIA HADN'T BEEN WAITING LONG. She had just left Tim, who had started a weekend stint at Mc-Donald's that would keep him occupied until six. They decided to eat in Arcadia again, and collected snacks and drinks on trays from a stand called Pizza-Face. Above the counter was an artist's impression of an all-singing, all-dancing pizza with bug eyes like a frog's and a gaping, grinning mouth. It was nearly enough to kill Joanne's appetite, and when she and Georgia took their places at a table, she made sure she was facing away from the stand.

Many of the tables were packed with squabbling children whose parents were yelling at them to shut up. More hungry shoppers, in a seemingly endless line, descended the mirrored escalators to the food stands that encircled the fountain. While they ate,

Joanne told Georgia about her encounter with Martin Wisemann. Georgia nodded, impressed, though his name meant nothing to her. "So you're going for older men these days," she joked, and Joanne tossed a plastic spoon at her. Then Joanne told her about Billy.

When she'd related the story, Georgia shook her head gravely. "I'm sorry. But then again, if you ask me, it's for the best. Billy's been such a jerk lately, I really can't see what's come over him."

"Jealousy, for one thing," Joanne said. "He was even jealous of *you*, for God's sake. It reached the point where he resented anything that didn't have to do with him. Sometimes, you know, he can be frightening. After that business on the bus today, I can't help wondering how serious he is; how far he'll go to get even."

"Get even for what? Come on, Jo, he brought this on himself."

Joanne shook her head. "That doesn't matter to him. You should've seen his face. I keep telling myself it's over now, it's all forgotten. But try telling it to Billy McGuire!"

Georgia smiled and took Joanne's hand. For several moments she said nothing. Briefly, Joanne was reminded of her sister Margaret—the pep talks she used to give before she left home, an answer for every love crisis. "You know what you need?" Georgia said.

"No. What?"

"For a start you need to calm yourself down and stop brooding. Half your problems are in your head. You're making things seem a hundred times worse by going over them and over them alone."

"Thank you, Ann Landers. You don't know how much that helps."

"I'm serious," Georgia said, letting Joanne's hand go. "Don't get me wrong. I'm not saying there's a right and a wrong way to do things, or that my way's the only way. I'm not saying there's anything wrong with being reclusive—"

"Reclusive!" Joanne almost shouted. "I see you every day, don't I? I'm here now, aren't I? I don't exactly lock myself away."

"You know what I mean. You keep yourself to yourself. Then you don't know how to ask for help when you need it."

"What are you getting at?" Joanne wanted to know.

"Nothing, really. Just telling you I'm here." Georgia paused, then smiled mischievously. "I'm also inviting you to Hazel's tonight. Her folks are away. We'll get drunk together. There'll be boy flesh in droves. Unattached boys!"

"How do you know that?"

"I don't know. It's wishful thinking."

Joanne gave in to laughter at last. Georgia had a habit of brightening her day when she needed it most. She sat back, breathing out, folding her arms in front of her. "What do you care, though? You've got Tim."

"That's not the point. The point is, will you come? Honestly, Jo, it's no big deal. Hazel's place is on Kingston Terrace, I think. That's not far from you, is it? If you hate it, you can walk home, no expense. Well?"

"All right." Joanne surrendered. "You've got me. I can't think of a single worthwhile excuse."

"Good! It's time you got that creep out of your system. Time you started thinking about somebody else."

"Anyone particular you have in mind?"

But Georgia just smiled.

It was almost four when Joanne thought of Martin Wisemann again. The town had vanished, to be replaced by country again. She had left Georgia at the perfume counter in Beales and hurried to the main bus station in time for the 48. A number of the passengers downstairs seemed tired and restrained because of the sun; one or two seemed barely alive at all. A man seated directly in front of Joanne turned a page of the local newspaper, and even that was an effort that took minutes. Someone upstairs was playing top forty, one vapid song after another. Oh, for cool jazz! She noticed a headline about vandalism— the cemetery story, probably—before the man folded his paper in half.

Wasn't that something she could mention to Martin? It might finally convince him to help her out. He'd asked if his stories had affected her in any way other than usual: Couldn't she tell him of her dream of the creature flitting down the tree in the cemetery, surely inspired by what she'd read in his book?

Either the sun had touched something off in her or Georgia had raised her spirits, or both; but suddenly she felt adventurous enough to go hunting for Martin Wisemann this minute. There were questions she wanted to ask, questions that couldn't wait a week. She remembered last night, the look of terror that had entered his eyes. Dare she ask him about that? Perhaps she should, to show how determined she was, how sincere. Surely he'd help her then. By the time she saw the signpost for Westbury and the bus stop beyond it, she had made up her mind.

What the hell: Why *not* go now? She wouldn't be expected at home yet. Saturdays were so often slack, everyone drifting in, eating, and drifting out as they pleased, Sarah running for a cheeseburger loaded with onions that would keep her awake all night, David stomping in late from Audiodrome and the pub.

She left the bus and started along the track, which was flanked by fields grown high with wheat and bright-yellow rape seed. A number of crows circled above the wheat field to her left. Ahead, she could see the beginnings of pine forestry, less distant than she remembered. She hoped she'd be welcome, arriving so soon. Perhaps Martin had made the invitation only to get rid of her. After all, he'd been anxious to escape from the moment they'd met. But if that was the case, he needn't have told her where he lived. He must have been sincere.

After the fields, the path continued over the humpbacked bridge where the stream had run dry, and on between the trees. The forestry had been hacked back over the year to enlarge the plantations, but the pines were still grouped so thickly that the light was excluded. Occasionally, odd rays of sunlight broke through to cast dappled patterns over the ripe forest floor. Here, the footpath became soft, even waterlogged in places, and there were tire tracks of various sizes and treads, overlapped and superimposed. Following the path, Joanne grew more and more aware of small, hurried movements everywhere about her. Several birds were turning up last winter's leaves and bracken in search of food; and a small shape, probably a squirrel, scurried along a branch above her.

Soon there was a brightness ahead, as though she were emerging from a tunnel. The day reaffirmed itself as the woodland petered out, and she caught her first glimpse of the cottages, grouped in the dip between the trees and the gently rising fells.

Her first thought, as she stood at the edge of the

trees looking down, was that she'd been time warped here. It was as if nothing had changed since her father had brought her to Westbury. The sound of silence was almost unbearable. Thin wisps of smoke rose from chimneys above the thatched roofs. Fruit trees flourished in all the private gardens. The white-painted outer walls appeared pristine, never touched. Only one building was obscured from this distance—the one her father had promised her, which was slightly set apart from the others. Hedgerows had grown up neglected around it, misshapen under their own weight; only the roof of the cottage was visible. There was no sign of smoke from its chimney. Although she had no way of knowing, she was strongly convinced the property was Martin's.

She set off down the slight incline toward it. At the bottom, stepping stones were dotted across a narrow, shallow stream where the water was not quite ankle deep. Tire tracks ended abruptly at one bank, began at the other. Joanne crossed over with three careful steps and approached the cottage. A rusting iron gate groaned as she pushed it open and stepped into the grounds.

Apart from the overgrown hedges and the lawn that needed cutting, it was much as she'd hoped it would be. No wonder she'd dreamed of owning a place like this. It was easy to see why an author would want to live here. She followed the gravel drive around to the front of the house, skirting the large expanse of lawn, in the center of which three chairs were drawn around a circular white iron table. There was a dried-up ornamental fountain and, at the far side of the lawn, a couple of outbuildings—a shed without windows and a wooden summerhouse built on a revolving platform, open on one side to the elements. There was no sign of Martin's VW.

She decided to try the back of the building. The yard there was less presentable, a tangle of nettles and high, rustling grass. If this was how Martin lived, he ought to have someone to take better care of him. Perhaps he couldn't afford a gardener now that he'd stopped publishing his writings. She hoped things would be tidier indoors.

What to do, though; leave now or wait? She stood in the silence, wondering. She had to stretch on her toes to see in through the downstairs window. The interior was dark, but she could still see the kitchen, bare but fairly presentable. Half a loaf of bread and a knife lay on a board beside the sink. A door stood half open across the room, but all she could make out was a grayish light beyond. Moving from the window, she tried the back door. Much to her surprise, she found it unlocked.

It seemed that an age had passed before she decided to go in. She'd come all this way, after all— would it really hurt if she looked inside for a minute? The door opened directly into the kitchen, and once it closed behind her, the silence seemed even more complete. The cottage sounded utterly dead, more than just empty. Perhaps solitude would be great for a while, but would she be able to stand so much of it?

The grayish light was coming from the end of the hall, through the tall frosted-glass panel beside the front door. She strode toward it until she reached the foot of the stairs on her left. Better not go up; that *would* be like prying. But which of the two closed doors, facing each other across the hall, should she take?

First, she tried the one on her right. It opened into a living room that was dominated by its book-lined walls. A couple of armchairs with lace coverlets draped over their backs were angled facing the old stone hearth, which was heaped with cold ashes. There was a framed photograph of an attractive, thirtyish woman on the mantelpiece. She noticed a shin-high coffee table, with an empty cup and several notebooks splayed across it and an ashtray overspilling with matches and butts beneath it. But the room felt cold, uninviting. There seemed no point in looking further.

She'd give Martin Wisemann five more minutes and then she would go. The other downstairs room was smaller and messier, littered with papers. It was, she saw quickly, his place of work. There seemed to be manuscripts everywhere, on the shelves and the floor; dogeared, bound with rubber bands, and built into skyscraper piles. A solid oak desk was pushed close to one wall, away from the direct sunlight. On it, surrounded by crumpled paper balls and hastily written memos, was an Olivetti electric typewriter, and beside that a telephone, the number an unlisted one, she guessed. Here too was the laden plastic shopping bag from the bookshop.

So he had returned home and gone again. Joanne felt a twinge of guilt as she went to the desk, smoothing a hand over its dusty surface. She was a trespasser, an invader of privacy, yet wasn't it strange, the sequence of events that had brought her here? Not one but *two* chance encounters with Martin—the writer she most admired—within a day of her cemetery dream, which his book had inspired in the first place; and the fact that, of all the houses he might have taken locally, it was this one, the one her father had promised her. If there was such a thing as fate, this was it. For whatever reason, she'd been meant to find Martin Wisemann.

So close to his work station, she couldn't resist actually sitting at it. She sat in the chair and inched forward, edging her knees under the desk, extending her legs. Then she ran her fingertips quickly, lightly over the typewriter keys. *It was coming up for air*, she typed absently. The touch-typing course she'd started this year was already paying dividends; she no longer had to watch the keys to know what she was doing. So this was how it felt to sit at an author's desk; but where did the ideas come from? Before she got up, she couldn't resist peeking inside the bag of books to see what Martin read privately. When she pulled the bag open, she gagged with surprise. Every single book was his own. *Nightstalk*, *Cold Comforts*, *Incubus*. It looked as though he'd cleared out the shop's entire stock, hardbacks and paperbacks alike.

Well, he must have his reasons. Most probably his own copies were damaged or worn out. Besides, it was his business, not hers. The five minutes she had given herself were up, and she ought to be going. As she stood, she saw Martin's wastebasket on the floor beside his desk. It was stuffed with discarded sheets, presumably from something he was currently working on. He'd said he still wrote, though he no longer published. Would it be too much of a liberty if she took a few pages as mementos? Surely he wouldn't miss them, or he wouldn't have thrown them away.

She drew out a handful of pages at random and smoothed them out on the desk. They were all covered with typing, and crossings out and handmade corrections in pencil, but the sheets were from two different pieces. Some were labeled "Cereal Killer" in the top right-hand corner; the rest were labeled "Dark Creation." The page numbers were all over the place, but it didn't matter if she had only part of the stories as keepsakes. If she could pluck up the courage to ask, Martin might let her read something more. She couldn't see why he'd object to one person reading what he'd done. But she wouldn't tell him about this. It felt a little like theft.

Satisfied with her find, she pushed the rest of the papers back into the wastebasket, folded and pocketed the ones she'd selected, and left the room. She had just set foot in the hall when she heard scampering noises above her head. Instinctively she looked up, but there was only the stuccoed ceiling and its single shaded bulb. What she'd heard had sounded like soft, rapid footsteps in one of the upstairs rooms. So she wasn't alone—but it couldn't be Martin up there, for where was his car?

Almost immediately the sounds began again, too rapid by far to be one set of footfalls, too lightweight to belong to anything human. Martin probably kept a pet dog or several cats, as Margaret did; that would explain it. But why would he keep them upstairs? Then the sounds ended and the silence returned, a silence she suddenly needed to escape from.

Her mouth was dry, her heart thick in her ears as she tried the front door for the quickest way out. The Yale lock turned easily, as did the handle, but the main key was missing. Martin would have it. She would have to go out the way she'd come in. As she reached the foot of the stairs, she heard more activity, followed by a cry of anger or pain, and she almost choked. She was sure she recognized the sound from somewhere, though it couldn't be a dog or a cat, let alone anything human. Although the cottage was in darkness, she could see the closed door at the top of the stairs. That was where the noises were. She thought she saw the door strain outward as something hammered against it from the other side.

She didn't wait to find out what it was. She had more than outstayed her welcome. A good half dozen strides took her to the kitchen, and then she was at the back door, straining at the handle.

At first she thought she was dreaming this too, for the door didn't seem to want to open. She'd seen films and read stories like this, where the exits were suddenly blocked; where the heroine—always stupid, always snooping where she shouldn't—would be trapped and left to the beast, or the raving psychotic, whichever. A sob of frustration rose to her throat. Upstairs, the sound of another impact rocked the woodwork. Then the latch gave with a rusty scrape, and she was out in the yard again.

Joanne backed slowly away, then fled around the side of the cottage. Birdsong was all there was to hear now. Even the neighbors were silent. Didn't they ever hang out laundry or stand chattering at their gates? Already it was hard to believe she'd heard anything inside—it was as though the cottage had fired her imagination—but she didn't intend to go back to make sure.

She didn't turn to look again until she reached the gate. From there, the cottage appeared as tranquil as ever. Ivy scaled the white walls; birds fluttered to and from the chimney like specks of soot. There was only one detail she had missed the first time she'd looked. Some of the upstairs windows were boarded up.

9

HAZEL FISHER SEEMED ALWAYS to be on the verge of
laughter or tears, so the parties she threw usually had
their moments. She was redheaded and fair skinned,
slim but large chested—Georgia claimed to be green-
eyed about that—and spoke in a rowdy sandpaper
voice that nobody envied. At the moment she was
also quite drunk. She was passing plates of crackers
and garlic bread to Joanne, who in turn was passing
them through the service hatch to the living room.
Joanne had to grab the plates quickly before Hazel
could drop them.

"I'm sorry," Hazel was slurring. "Sorry, I mean,
that this isn't what you expected. The party's a flop."

"No it isn't," Joanne assured her. "It's early yet.
You just wait."

"But there are no *boys*. It's like a freakin' hen

party. We'll all end up sitting cross-legged on the floor again. And singing those Simon and Garfunkel songs again, with me being asked to play the guitar." She frowned at Joanne as though having difficulty focusing. "Don't you just *hate* it when only the girls turn up?"

"Not me," Georgia said. She was straddling a back-to-front pine chair and sipping a tequila sunrise in which the sun had set. On the table beside her were several glasses filled with red wine. "We girls don't do this often enough. There's nothing quite like getting together for a good, old-fashioned heart to heart."

"And a bitch," Joanne added.

"Yes, and that," Georgia said.

"But you brought Tim," Hazel complained. "What about me? I told Andy about this weeks ago and he *still* couldn't make it. He said he was having to work late again, but I don't know. Sometimes, I just don't know. I hate all-night takeout stands. And what about you?" she went on, turning on Joanne, tears blurring her eyes again. "You're *completely* alone now, aren't you? And there's no one here, no boys for you to meet. God, I feel so terrible."

Joanne smiled and collected her drink from beside the service hatch, another of Georgia's blushing tequila sunrises. "Don't worry about it," she said to Hazel. "Honestly, there are other things in life. And besides, there's always the danger I might meet a true dud on the rebound."

"That's the spirit," Georgia said loudly, and slapped her thigh. Even Georgia was slurring a little now. "Will you please stop worrying on everyone's behalf, Hazel? Joanne came because she wanted to; she didn't come to pair off, did you Joanne?"

"I came because Georgia told me there'd be wall-to-wall boy flesh," Joanne said dryly, and Hazel's tears became laughter at a stroke.

It was one of those good-mannered evenings where you could hear yourself think above the sounds. No one seemed to care which music was played. In the living room, a blond girl Joanne didn't know was putting on a record without checking the label. Tim was one of only four males to have arrived, and the others were spoken for; to Joanne's knowledge he had already been approached by two girls, and each he had sent away with a kind word and a hunch of the shoulders. He was wearing a black shirt with beige chinos and nut-brown oxfords. Another girl was eyeing him with interest as Joanne followed Georgia to the living room.

Georgia was in her element. "He's all *mine*, and they can't have him, just think of it!" she said, steering Joanne toward an empty leather sofa, then thrusting an arm about Joanne's shoulders. "Seriously, are you really okay? I know there's nothing quite like a crowd to make you feel lonely as hell."

"What crowd?" Together they sank into the sofa,

which was flanked by twin rubber plants. Seated, Joanne said, "No, that's all right. This is enough to cheer anyone up, don't you think?" She gestured around the room at the dozen or so party guests trying hard to fill the space. Among them was a girl in a red leather jacket who had found Hazel's acoustic guitar behind one of the armchairs.

"Uh-oh, spare me," Georgia said, and flung herself up again. "Time to see if the little girl's room is free."

She had been gone no more than a few seconds when the Simon and Garfunkel songs began, and the records were promptly turned off. Joanne sat back, cringing, sipping her drink. It still seemed early for the party to have degenerated into singsong. After a minute she noticed Tim watching her with a smile from across the room. Saluting her with his glass, making excuses to the girl who was trying to talk to him, he came over.

"You seem to be in demand tonight," Joanne said as he flopped on the sofa beside her.

"It's just that I'm a minority here," he said modestly.

"Well, Georgia doesn't seem to mind. Anyone else would have been seething."

"Georgia's different, though. She's great. You know, I get the feeling she really appreciates me."

"She does."

"I can't imagine what for."

"Perhaps that's why," Joanne suggested. "You don't go around wasting everyone's time trying to prove to them how special you are."

They were silent for a minute, gazing away from each other to the group that was forming about the girl with the guitar. Some were singing, some humming along to "Scarborough Fair." Most of the words were a blur. One of the audience was lighting a joint, the air quickly filling with its sour, pungent odor.

Tim shook his head, unimpressed, and turned back to Joanne. "Georgia tells me you bumped into that writer today, Martin Wisemann."

"That's right. You know Carleton's, the bookshop? He was there. He'd been buying up copies of all his own books," she said, and quickly downed what was left of her drink to stop herself from saying more; she wasn't supposed to know so much.

Tim said, "That's odd," but seemed happy to leave the matter there. "You know, I *thought* I'd seen him around town once or twice—in Smith's, and Sherratt and Hughes, I think—but I couldn't be sure it was him. So he's really living near here?"

"Yes, in Westbury. I—" Again she faltered, her parting image of the cottage still unbearably vivid in her mind. "—I'm supposed to go out there soon, to meet him. I'm hoping to base my English assignment on his work, and I'm trying to get him to participate."

"That would be something, if he did," Tim said.

"Yes, it would."

"You might ask him why he hasn't brought out a new book in—how long is it now?"

"Ten years."

"Ten years? Since his wife died, I expect. That would explain it."

The comment was a throwaway, but Joanne was suddenly sitting bolt upright, fingers tensing around her glass. "What was that you said?"

"About what? His wife?" Tim shrugged matter-of-factly. "There was really nothing to it. It was something I picked up from one of the Sunday color supplements—one of those 'Where Are They Now' features, you know the kind. And Wisemann was mentioned in the article; all I remember is that his wife had died in an accident of some kind—it didn't go into detail—and that he hadn't been heard of since. There was conjecture about how much some publisher or other was willing to pay him to write again, but it didn't seem likely he would."

"Was there anything else?"

"No, I don't think so. I only remember that because I was reading a lot of his stuff at the time, *Incubus* I think, and *Nightstalk*. Bloody good novels, I thought. Or should that be good and bloody?"

"He never mentioned a wife when I asked him why he quit writing," Joanne murmured, thinking aloud. "Could she be the reason he's stopped?"

"Well, maybe you didn't ask. Exactly how long did you spend with him anyway?"

"Five minutes, if that."

"There you are then. You'll have to know him better than that, won't you, before you start asking personal questions."

"I suppose so." Joanne nodded and relaxed again. All at once she wanted to be free of company and alone again, poring over Martin's books, fitting together the events of the last few days. A picture was trying to emerge—she could be certain of that—but as yet it was only a jumble of colors and lines that didn't quite meet where they should. God, she wished she could simply enjoy herself here—kick off her shoes and drink too much and get high—but it was as though something had taken hold of her; something that wanted to come first, excluding all else.

She must have been sitting and drifting in thought for several instants before Tim nudged her back to herself. "Why so down at the mouth, Jo? Is it because your glass is so empty or because the party's so lousy? Give it here, I'll fetch you a refill."

"I'll come with you," she said, getting up, side-stepping a girl who had fallen asleep on the floor. She took Tim's arm as they walked through the debris. Above the drunken song she heard a door slam somewhere in the house, then several male voices all talking at once. Nearing the kitchen, she caught a glimpse of Hazel through the service hatch, looking blearily up from her seat at the table. But Hazel didn't see Joanne; behind her, someone had entered the kitchen.

"Well, it looks like things are on the up and up," Hazel called to no one in particular. Then her face seemed to change.

"I wouldn't bank on it," Joanne said, because Billy McGuire was standing in the doorway between the living room and kitchen, Heineken six-pack in hand. In the kitchen behind him were two of his friends, their clothes held together by fraying patches. He stared at Joanne, then at Tim, his features gradually forming a leer. "Well well," he said thickly. "Well well."

"Oh God," Joanne heard Georgia exclaim somewhere to her right. "This is all we need."

She felt her hand slide from Tim's arm as she returned Billy's gaze. She hoped he could see how little Tim meant to her. His eyes were aglow with madness; a corner of his mouth ticked. She said coolly, "How did you find out about this?"

"Walls have ears. Not welcome here, am I, is that it?"

"Spare us the trouble, Billy, please," she said, but Billy came back at her, "Trouble, what trouble? Is that what you think I'm here for?"

"Be honest: What other reason would you have?"

"We've something to discuss, you and me," he

said. "Or have you forgotten already?" He gestured at Tim as though Tim were a turd on the carpet. "Is this how you've been passing your time, then? Does he know about the old fart you tried to pick up at the bookshop? Didn't think *I* knew about that, did you, but I saw you well enough. I know what you're up to, I know your sort. Didn't take you long to recover from the *upset*, did it? What's this creep got that I haven't, tell me that."

"We're just friends," Joanne said. "But friendship's a damn sight more than I ever got from you."

She was turning away from him and toward the door across the living room that adjoined the hall, when Billy took hold of her arm. "I haven't finished with you yet," he said.

"Well I have with you." In the heat of the moment she was vaguely aware of the Simon and Garfunkel sing-along stopping; of faces turning toward her in the smoke. But she felt no embarrassment; let them all see her anger—let them see what Billy McGuire was about. Dry mouthed, she seethed at him, "Will you leave me alone now! There's nothing I want to say to you! If you don't stop pushing me right this minute, I'll—"

"What?" Billy said gleefully. "You'll what?"

"She'll nothing, but you'll leave her alone all the same."

Momentarily, everything seemed to stop dead.

Joanne heard a gathering of breath around the room. The words were Tim's. He stood, feet planted slightly apart, fists gathered uncertainly at his sides. His tongue poked nervously between his lips for a second, then vanished. Billy McGuire laughed loudly, forcedly, and then stopped abruptly. Now he was studying Tim with renewed interest: no longer a turd but a delicacy, to be swallowed down with one swift gulp.

After a second Joanne said, "Don't get involved, Tim. This is just between us." To Billy she said, "Let go of my arm or someone will call the cops." But someone already was. Through the open hallway door she saw Georgia, muttering into the telephone. As she pulled against Billy in an effort to free herself, Billy wrenched her back, hard enough to make her cry out.

It was as if something snapped in Tim at that point. He couldn't be a fighter—she had never so much as overheard him in an argument with anyone—but he launched himself forward with a ferocity that surprised her. His palm caught Billy McGuire full in the chest, spinning the six-pack loose from one hand while freeing Joanne from the other. Joanne stumbled clear, three or four paces, as Billy tumbled sideways into the doorjamb, a look of utter surprise on his face. Slowly the look was replaced by one of contempt. After that, Tim seemed to run out of ideas, and dropped his arms back to his sides. Joanne was right: He wasn't a fighter, he wouldn't be capable of pushing this further.

"Better get out of here," he said quietly to Joanne. "I'll be right behind you." The next second he was on the carpet, tumbled roughly aside as Billy brushed past him and went after Joanne. "Teach him a lesson," Joanne heard Billy call to his friends as she backed into the hall.

Georgia already had the front door open. Joanne passed through it, along Hazel's drive, and into the floodlit street before looking back. The single yellow rectangle of doorway looked crammed with a confusion of bodies caught in a scuffle. There were shouts and cries and the sound of glass breaking. Georgia must be in the thick of it. She ought to go back and help, she thought, and then she saw the group of figures bursting outdoors and along the driveway toward her, their footfalls as loud as guns.

There were five, perhaps six of them in all. There was no time to decide what to do, which way to turn. Everything seemed to slow, and she became vividly aware of upstairs lights flickering on in the neighboring houses. Confusion and fear held her rigid.

"Move yourself!" someone screamed at her— Georgia, of course, with Tim running close at her heels. Clearing the gateway, they veered away to Joanne's right, in the direction of Gower Lane. It was the wrong end of the street for Joanne, but the urgency of Georgia's shout helped her move. Without another thought she took off in the opposite direction. Behind her, three more figures had reached the gateway and hastily separated. Two were giving chase to Georgia and Tim; the third—it could only be Billy McGuire—was pounding along the pavement behind Joanne.

He must be crazy, there must be something *wrong* with him. Could he seriously believe he'd win her back with behavior like this? No, she thought, even he would know they were past the point of no return. He could have only one reason for following her now, and that was to hurt her.

Please God please let the cops arrive quickly! She had about two hundred yards to the end of the street, before the alley connecting with Fairview Road. After that, there'd be only the straight path past the cemetery and home. If she could just maintain this pace, she thought, but already her throat and chest were aflame, her heart like a weapon being used against her. This was what sitting around reading books did for you! She had let all her stamina drain away; her body was next to useless. There was no need to glance back to know that Billy was gaining. The closeness of his tread, the harsh gasp of his breath was enough. As she ran, leafy hedgerows clawed at her face across collapsed garden walls. She flashed them aside with a hand, ducked from a low-hanging tree branch, and for an instant was so preoccupied with shielding her eyes, she forgot where her feet were landing.

It was either a pothole or the curb's edge. She felt herself go over on an ankle, felt the shock of hard ground skinning her palms as she landed, heard the scrape of his shoes pulling up. When she'd recovered sufficiently to scramble to her knees, Joanne saw Billy's outline above her, his shadow trailing off between the gateposts of a garden that looked thick with privet hedges and head-high conifers. He stood between the posts, in the orange haze of a streetlamp, but she couldn't see his face, which was masked by the dark. For a time there was silence—except for her beating heart, the stirring of foliage behind Billy.

Finally he said, "I told you I wouldn't let you get away with it. I don't give up easily. No one treats me the way you've treated me."

She couldn't run, for the fall had winded her, ending her hopes of escape. The only thing now was to buy time, hope he calmed down. Still on her knees, she said, "All right, you win. I can see there's no point in arguing, Billy. But can we please talk this out tomorrow? I'm not in the best frame of mind to—"

"No," he cut her short. "No, there'll be no more talk, not from you anyway. I know what you're about now. You were playing me along like all the others."

"What others?"

"You can't pull the wool over my eyes. I'll bet you were cheating from the start, leading me on. Does he know what you are, that jerk you were with tonight, that Tim?"

"I told you already, he's just a friend, nothing more. I told you—"

"And you're just a bitch who needs to be taught a lesson, and no one should trust you, no one should—"

"Billy, please," she began, but his silhouette had turned sharply away from her. Incredibly, he was going to leave her alone, having said all he had to; she must have misjudged him after all. That, at least, was her first thought. It was what she would have liked to believe. She didn't immediately realize he had turned, not from her, but because of what he'd heard close behind him. Seconds later he was screaming, though the sounds were quickly muffled. She understood why all too soon.

Somewhere, at some other time, she had witnessed this scene before. She ought to have noticed how familiar everything was—the quality of light in the street, the surge of activity behind Billy. Hadn't someone included a scene like this in the movie trailer she'd sat through only last night? But of course—the movie was adapted from *Nightstalk*; no wonder she'd felt she had seen it before. In which case she knew what came next.

She had to be mistaken, she prayed she was. Even

when something came roaring out of the dark toward Billy, she hoped to be wrong. Above all she hoped that soon she would faint, or wake up perspiring from another dream. Only a dream could explain the conifer uprooting itself from the shadows and soil beside the drive. It was only at the last that she realized it wasn't a tree at all; it was no more a tree than this was a dream. For the branch that seized Billy McGuire from behind was someone's left arm, while the right hand that was raised held a knife.

10

BY THE TIME SHE REACHED Fairview Road, her mind
was reeling. Only a miracle could have brought her
this far, this fast. It was a wonder she'd managed to
pick herself up, let alone escape at full pelt. Now her
head throbbed painfully. Everywhere around her the
streetlamps formed prisms of light; but the noise in
her head was not so pretty. A man's angry voice and
a car horn competed. In her haste, she had stepped
into the face of the traffic. Any other time the sight
of the car braking sharply would have shocked her.
Not now though, not tonight; she'd gone beyond
shock. At least the car's horn was loud enough to
drown the sound in her head; the after-echo of Billy
McGuire's scream.

Crossing over, she turned breathlessly into Peterborough Lane, not waiting to hear what the motorists

were shouting now. A small stealthy shape tracked her along the cemetery gates as she ran—her shadow. Someone had vandalized the main gate, she saw; the padlock had been shattered as if with a hammer. She looked stubbornly away, toward home. She didn't want to think about gateways or gateposts. She needed to be free of her last image of Billy; of the moment he was wrenched into darkness beside the drive.

She was almost in tears—from the shock, from the physical pain of falling and running—as she grappled with her key on its beer-barrel key ring and fitted it to the lock. Thankfully, all the lights were out, everyone having turned in. She wouldn't have to contend or explain. If only Georgia were here, though, to be with and talk with! She wished for days, not too long ago, when they had slept at each other's houses, in each other's beds, sharing their secrets in whispers. Was it too late to call Georgia, to make sure she and Tim had arrived home safely? Who else could she speak to about tonight?

She went to the phone and lifted the receiver. On the pad was a memo in Sarah's heavy, determined handwriting.

Joanne, it read, *someone called for you while you were out and I told them you were at Hazel's and I asked if they had a message for you but they hadn't.* Sarah's messages were all of this kind, written as she spoke, without pauses for breath. The caller had probably been Billy, which at least explained how he'd known where to find her. After a minute Joanne tapped out Georgia's number and let it ring ten or twelve times before hanging up. No doubt she'd woken Georgia's folks, but surely this was more important than anyone's good night's sleep. She thought of trying the number again, but decided against it. Better to see Georgia in person tomorrow, give herself time to be clear about what had happened. In recent times she had seen things, sensed things, that could only be born of imagination. But the figure in the driveway had been real tonight, just as Billy McGuire's cry had been real.

She should have stayed and helped him, done what she could—but it was easy to think boldly after the fact, and in any case she would only have perished with him. She trod upstairs, heavily, wearily, knowing exhaustion wouldn't lead her to sleep. In the darkened bedroom she undressed and put on her nightgown with ritual slowness, turned on her radio-cassette player as low as it would go, and fell into bed. Almost immediately she sensed the dark pressing down on her, and she flipped on the bedside light.

Should she have called the police, or had the incident been less serious than it seemed at the time? Come on, though, Joanne, the figure had wielded a *knife* for God's sake. Just how serious did a thing have to be?

87

She lay for a while with the radio on. It was tuned to a late-night phone-in show, but the sound was so low she heard little of anything being said. In any case the host was usually so full of his own opinions, so smug and impatient with everyone who called, that the whole thing seemed a pointless wallow, a bitch for the sake of a bitch. Remarkably, she had drifted half to sleep—tonight, she hadn't expected sleeping at all—when a thought made her sit up sharply.

Why did everything seem to revolve around Martin? Could someone have read his novel *Nightstalk*, or watched the film based upon it, before acting out the scene she had witnessed tonight? Maybe that was why it had been so familiar. She could think of no other reason. She remembered Miss Rees two weeks ago in English, speaking of life imitating art. And there were psychos in every large and small community who were only too willing to steal their ideas from all the best movies and books. Check out the six-o'clock news every day, and there they were.

But none of this explained why, in the midst of the evening's chaos, it was Martin Wisemann who bothered her. It was as if the madness of recent times had multiplied since she first set eyes on him.

Even now, she could see the expression on his face. And then there were the books he had bought— surely nothing odd about that in itself, not unless you then considered his wife, or the ten long years since the last book he'd published. And then there were the noises upstairs in the cottage. Until the last hour, she might have dismissed that as imagination too. Why was it, though, that all of these items seemed part of whatever was happening—part of something so large she couldn't quite see the whole picture, perhaps because she was part of it? Surely, a killing straight from the pages of *Nightstalk* was more than coincidence. Had to be.

Good grief, sleep was definitely out, by the looks of it. Though her body was crying for rest, her mind was alert. She pushed aside the bedsheets, threw on her terry robe, and was half out of the room before she remembered the pages she'd taken from Martin's cottage. She hadn't read them yet, but perhaps, being works in progress, they would shed some light on one or two issues.

She sat at the kitchen table, scanning the pages, a cup of hot chocolate steaming at her elbow. There wasn't enough material here to be positive, but the little she had read seemed unconnected with tonight's events. These were stories, nothing more. A little weirder and wilder than his earlier work, but certainly vintage Wisemann. The first, "Cereal Killer"—she'd initially thought it a misspelling of "serial"—was astonishing. In it, for whatever reason, none other than Honey Monster had found a way to break loose from the Sugar Puffs box that held him captive and had gone on the rampage, biting the heads off three breakfasting children before—well, before whatever happened, happened. At this point, the pages ran out.

The idea was so wild she felt heartened. At least it proved she could still be uplifted. The second of the stories was "Dark Creation," on one page of which a girl was doing battle with something she had locked in a basement, and which had multiplied and grown behind the door. Another page was set in a theater or cinema, but there wasn't enough here to be clear what was taking place; perhaps Martin would tell her the rest, if she dared contact him after today. The page numbers suggested a novel, not a short story. It seemed a shame that so much time and effort should be expended when he had no intention of publishing. There, again, was another question that bothered her. Why should he be compelled to keep writing and revising, when he knew damn well it was only for him?

Finally, none the wiser, she straightened the pages and pushed them from her. In the street outside there were headlights, and the sound of a car pulling up and doors thumping shut. It was late—almost two, much later than she usually stayed up. Even so, she found herself heading to the front door almost as a matter of course, as if she were expecting someone.

So who *am* I expecting? she wondered, turning the key, sweeping open the door. She might have been enacting a scene from another story, though she couldn't place which one. On the doorstep, facing her, a uniformed policeman held a fist in midair, caught in the act of knocking. Beside him was a policewoman, also in uniform, with a round, pale, unsmiling face. It was she who spoke first.

"Is there a Joanne Towne living here?"

"Yes," Joanne told her. "There is . . . I mean, that's me."

"I'm afraid we have to ask you some questions," the policewoman said. "Do you know anyone by the name of McGuire? William McGuire?"

The sudden chill air caused Joanne to clutch at herself. She fumbled as she pulled her robe tightly about her, and was surprised to hear tears in her voice when she spoke.

"You'd better come in," she told them.

11

THE WEATHER IMPROVED notably with each passing day. Clouds climbed higher and grew softer, the wind dropped, even the sky itself lost its former milky complexion. In the backyards beneath the clotheslines, girls laid out towels and air beds on the patios and settled back to commune with the sun. Farther afield, in the parks and local playing fields, kids swarmed like bees, formed gangs, and fought and played soccer, making the most of their vacation.

Soon it would be over. Joanne couldn't avoid the feeling she'd allowed the time to slip through her fingers. Now she was farther than ever from Martin; it no longer seemed possible to visit Westbury, for even if she'd had the courage, she didn't now have the time. Miss Rees, thank God, was easy about unfinished projects. She would pout, screw up her nose, and give Joanne several more days to complete the task. Perhaps Joanne should choose someone more conventional to study, Graham Greene or John Steinbeck. Either would be fine by Miss Rees, preferable in her eyes to Martin, but neither lived locally, and neither had written anything that remotely compared with "Cereal Killer."

Where had the days gone? She had tried to keep Billy McGuire out of her thoughts by busying herself in trivial ways. Following her mother and Jason around the house, cleaning dishes and emptying ashtrays, emptying and replacing the vacuum cleaner bag, checking that the hose and nozzle were clear. Once or twice she had met with Georgia, once with Georgia and Tim together. They had all sat in silence at the wine bar one night, a silence no one had seemed able to shift. It was still too close and too painful to ignore. A drink or two or three couldn't change anything. At night she had wanted to read, and yet something—a fear she couldn't quite pinpoint—had stopped her. It was as though she'd been afraid of becoming too involved with the characters and plot, of having to relive the nightmare.

So it was Thursday, midday and days later, as she leaned from her window, the sun in her face, and watched the slow procession of limos far across the cemetery. The silence was so acute, it seemed for a moment the world had stopped turning. Eventually the cars pulled up like a train at a platform, the pall-bearers and mourners forming an orderly line that progressed even more slowly on foot through the gates at the far side. The coffin-shaped hole, mounds of earth at its edges, waited on the near side, beneath a tree quite close to the main entrance. Why hadn't the funeral cars drawn up in Peterborough Lane, if the ceremony was to take place so near to it? Probably because the long, silent walk to the grave site was such a necessary ordeal.

All flesh is grass, Joanne thought. The grass withers, the flower fades . . . She closed her eyes respectfully for a minute, then opened them again as she heard the door behind her.

"Jo?" It was Georgia, standing in the doorway. "Your mom let me in. Is it all right if I join you?"

"Sure." Joanne didn't move from the window. Georgia came around beside her. Joanne said, "I was just watching—"

"I can see. Don't you think one funeral is enough for one week? Do you have to put yourself through it all again?"

Joanne shrugged. She felt nothing. Two days ago she had stood with Georgia at Billy's grave, wringing her hands, wishing she were able to cry uncontrollably as some of the others were crying, as if that would prove she cared. Perhaps she was still too numb for tears.

The mourners were filing languidly around the grave site. Somewhere above them, a bird burst startled from its tree. Twenty yards back along the path, the bland mound where Billy rested was clearly visible. Joanne said, "Do you think they'll blame me for what happened?"

"Who?"

"Billy's folks. Now that the whole story is out. Do you think they'll hold me responsible?"

"God, no." Georgia sounded appalled. "What kind of lunatic idea is that?"

"I don't know. I thought about calling them, before, to try and explain. Last night I even picked up the phone, but I couldn't dial. Whatever I said would have sounded bad. However you try and explain it, it boils down to one thing: me leading Billy into the path of the killer."

"You mustn't *think* like that," Georgia said. "He led himself into it, and that's a fact. I know how you're feeling right now, but don't forget what happened there. We were *all* running for our lives, weren't we? Any one of us would have been in serious trouble if we'd been caught."

"Yes, but—"

"Yes but nothing. There's no avoiding the fact that Billy gate-crashed the party because he was looking for trouble, and trouble's just what he got. There were enough people, *sober* people, at Hazel's to confirm what we told the police. Everyone saw what Billy was doing. It's impossible to tell it any other way."

Joanne nodded and fell respectfully silent. Georgia was right, and she knew it. It was time she stopped blaming herself. At the head of the grave, a young deaconess began reading solemnly. As she did so, the sound of distant traffic seemed to fade. Her voice, a dull monotone, barely carried; the words were unclear. To Joanne, it seemed an age had passed since she'd first been attracted to Billy, said yes when he'd nervously invited her out; and now he was nothing, a memory, another monster thrown up in her path to haunt her.

At last Joanne turned from the window, sat down on the bed, hands together. "Will you stay for a while?" she asked Georgia, who was studying the book-heavy shelves with vacant uninterest. "I'd appreciate the company."

Georgia pulled a book from the shelf—*Into the Void*—and looked at it once before pushing it back. "I'll stay, but not here. You need a change from this place, Jo."

It was Georgia, after lunch, who suggested the park. For the hell of it, they agreed to take Sarah and Jason. Joanne couldn't fail to notice her mother's relief when Georgia made the offer. She had reached her fortieth birthday in March, a point of no return, as she called it. Trying to keep pace with Jason had added another line to her brow, another few gray hairs to her scalp. And now the news of Billy and the wait for more news about Mary were also taking their toll, and there was a weary and slightly jaded look about her, as if she were verging on sleep. When they left, she was settled in the living room with James Clavell, six hundred pages still to go.

"If you're really good, both of you, you can have ice creams," Joanne told Sarah and Jason later.

Sarah said, "Tell that to Jason. I'll have one anyway—I saved up."

Joanne hunched her shoulders at Georgia. "You see what I have to put up with?"

Georgia smiled sympathetically. "Life is hell, isn't it?"

They were on a bench at lakeside. To the north, about a quarter mile away, were the tennis courts and hothouse gardens. South were the putting greens, patchy and brown after months of extended use. Everywhere Joanne looked, couples her own age roamed, arm in arm, and stopped to gaze meaningfully into each other's eyes. What had she seen in Billy's eyes during those last few days? But for weeks she hadn't dared look.

"Look," Jason said, breaking into her thoughts and pointing. Families of ducks were drifting across the oval lake; some were stopping to shake themselves on the small dark island rising like a giant's back from the center. The sound of water was pleasant, lulling. "Look, look, look!"

"Yes," Joanne told him. "Yes, yes, yes." She hadn't mastered the art of conversing with Jason yet. She watched him crawl and fall, go scurrying away to be picked up by Sarah, who brought him back legs dangling in midair to the bench. "Not too rough with him," Joanne warned, but Jason was giggling.

"See? You're looking better already," Georgia said. Today she had on a white T-shirt and jeans, which, with her short-cropped hair and Ray-Ban sunglasses, gave her the look of a screen starlet, or at least a TV model. "Didn't I tell you your problems were right there in your head? And with being cooped up in your room?"

"Problems?" Joanne laughed. "What problems?"

"That's what I like to hear." Georgia flinched as Jason climbed onto the bench and groped her. Helping him into a sitting position, she pointed across the water. "There's a swan, a swan, you see?" To Joanne, "Did you do any more with your project yet?"

"Not yet."

"Well, you should. It would be the best thing for you. Do I sound like your nanny?"

"A little."

"Who cares if I do? I know this is brutal, but Billy is *gone*, and you have to find better ways of occupying yourself. Unless I'm mistaken, Martin Wisemann actually *invited* you to his place, didn't he?"

"He did."

"Then why aren't you there with him this minute instead of here with me?"

Joanne shook her head. "It's a long story."

"Well, I've got until six, when Tim gets off. I thought this was exactly what you'd been waiting for. Can't you imagine how sappy everyone's project will look when you walk in with an actual interview? Tim says there are people in the national press who'd die to have what you've got."

"In what sense?"

"In the sense that they're still asking 'Where Is He Now?' As far as they know, Wisemann is a missing person; has been for ten years. Honestly, Jo, you don't know what you're onto. You thought it was only an English assignment when it's actually a leading newspaper story!"

Joanne took a moment to consider this. Sarah was walking away, toward the ice cream stand. "Then why me?" Joanne said.

"Why you?"

"Yes, why me? If Martin wants never to be found, why should he talk to me? He could just as easily have told me to jump in the lake, but instead he agreed to meet."

"Perhaps it's because you're a genuine reader," Georgia suggested. "You're interested in *him*, not in how newsworthy he is. Perhaps it was love at first sight. Who knows? What matters is you're wasting a wonderful chance as long as you're sitting around feeling sorry for Billy or yourself or whoever else happens to cross your thoughts. Whoops!—I'm sounding like Ann Landers again!"

She was absolutely right. Hearing Georgia say it aloud was something she'd badly needed. It was like therapy, like hearing her own confession to a feeling of instantaneous relief. Joanne closed her eyes for a minute and felt tension leaving her, step by step. Behind her lids the world had assumed an orange-pink hue; not at all as gray and black and shades in between as she'd thought.

Minutes came and went as she sat there, floating. In the end she said, "Right, you're on. I'll go back there as soon as I can."

"Meaning what? You've been there already? Are you holding out on me, Towne? What have you been up to?"

Ah, she'd made the slip! She might as well tell the rest now that she felt able to. Until now, her experience at the cottage had been a private ordeal. She hadn't intended to mention it because she'd gone in like a thief, uninvited. But perhaps keeping it to herself had made things more difficult, and perhaps it would help if she shared what she knew. Describing her visit to Westbury made her feel as a storyteller must feel: glad to be rid of the burden at last. She wondered if that was why Martin still worked— because the stories were still there, weighing him down, just waiting to be gotten rid of.

When she'd finished, Georgia whistled appreciatively and said, "And the windows were really boarded up?"

"Yes, the upstairs ones were."

"What do you suppose he is keeping up there? A wild animal of some kind? A roomful of rats?"

"I'm only telling you what I *thought* I heard. I could've been mistaken. After all, there have been other things lately, and I thought that after the upset with Billy—"

"What other things?" Joanne felt Georgia's weight shift on the bench. "What else have you been hearing?"

"Not hearing, seeing. Remember the accident outside the Arcadia Center last week? It was because someone—something—ran out into the traffic. It all happened so quickly, but I would have sworn—"

"Yes? You would have sworn what?"

"It won't make any sense. I would have sworn that whatever caused that car to swerve was, well, not quite human."

"You're kidding."

"I wish I were, I really do."

For a time there was a silence between them; silence and the sun on Joanne's closed eyes, and the feeling of peace about to be broken. She imagined, briefly, how it would be to open her eyes and see a hundred faces staring down, waiting intently on her next words. But it was Georgia who said, "Is there any chance you were wrong? Did anyone else see what you saw?"

"I don't think so. Except perhaps—" She paused, wondering, uncertain. "Martin was there. He wasn't there long. He told me he'd hurried away because he hated the way crowds stared, but I saw his face and I *know* there was more to it than that."

Georgia considered for a moment, then said, "Nothing seems to connect, does it? There's Wisemann in the center of things, with everything happening around him. And there's you."

"And I'm afraid," Joanne said. "That's why I haven't been back to see him; it doesn't only have to do with Billy. It's as if I'm being drawn into something against my will."

"But what?"

"Something bad. Something too close for comfort."

Her words hung in the air for a second. They were a hard act to follow, but she'd made her point clearly now. Something was closing in on her, and had been for some time. Suddenly she was gagging for a cool drink, something to take the dryness away. She heard a child's cry in the distance, and had recognized the urgent tone before the single, repeated word made sense.

"Jo-*anne*! Jo-*anne*!"

The voice was Sarah's. Joanne opened her eyes, and the pale moderate colors were replaced by dazzle. Before she had properly focused, she heard Georgia gasp into her open-palmed hand. Jason stood at the water's edge, bending and reaching toward his death.

The bench rocked violently as she and Georgia took to their feet. A hundred yards distant, rounding the lakeside on the left, Sarah dropped two ice cream cones and began running.

"Stop him, Jo, stop him!"

Georgia was there first, however. In the same instant Jason stepped into space, she caught him firmly beneath both arms and brought him sweeping back to safety. Water dribbled from his right leg; beneath him, a swirl of ripples formed on the surface as if something had just gone under. At the very edge of the concrete bank, Joanne saw a wet print like a duck's tread.

"My God," Georgia said, nursing Jason. "How could we be so neglectful?" She was looking at Joanne as though the answer to that was a terrible secret they shared.

"We'll have to be more careful in the future," Joanne said. She stood there breathing hard while the others walked back toward the bench. Yes, she would have to take much greater care. Dropping down on her haunches, she dipped a hand into the water. Behind her she heard Sarah calling, "You owe me two cones, Jo—don't think you're getting away with it."

Joanne didn't answer immediately. She was wondering why the duck that Jason had reached for hadn't surfaced. Ripples dispersed as the water grew calm. When nothing came up, she looked farther afield. The nearest birds were some distance away, thirty or forty yards or more, but he couldn't have been reaching for anything else. The print at her feet could only have been a duck's or a swan's; not what she'd thought at first. From a certain angle, it looked much like the small but webbed handprint of a man.

12

IT WAS DAVID WHO UNEXPECTEDLY opened the door when they reached home. He should have been at work, but Joanne quickly guessed from his face that something was wrong. No sooner had they stepped inside than Joanne saw her mother come thumping down the stairs in her coat, a cigarette cocked in her left hand, an overnight bag loading down her right.

"Jo, I have to ask you a favor." Reaching the hall, she stubbed out the cigarette in the ashtray next to the phone. "There was a call from your uncle Ted."

"I'd better be going," Georgia said tactfully.

Joanne gave her a brief, firm hug and a peck on the cheek. "Thanks," she said softly, and looking sideways at Jason, "for everything."

"Don't mention it. I'll see you tomorrow."

When the door closed after Georgia, Joanne's

mother sighed. "The news is not good. They have her in intensive care now. David has agreed to drive down with me, but it's at least two hours away. We may have to stay for a couple of days."

"I see." Joanne gave Jason's hair a ruffle, and Jason went waddling to the living room, where seconds later something crashed. "You want me to take charge."

"Could you?" Her mother looked anxious, desperate not to impose. "It's just that the journey and the circumstances—well, if I thought it would be all right to take him, I would. But I know he'll be fine with you; I realize it's a terrific responsibility."

You said it, Joanne thought, and then sensed that Sarah was staring. "We'll cope splendidly, won't we brat?"

"If you'll stop calling me that, we might."

"It's just," her mother went on, "that I know it's your last few days before school. I know how you planned to use your time. But I'll make it up to you, I promise."

"Whatever else happens, we'll be back by Sunday," David said, taking the bag from her mother to carry outside.

"Don't forget Margaret if you need anything," her mother said. "I've already spoken to her, and she's free to help out while we're gone." After a breath she continued. "There's money under the clock in the living room, but you'll have to take care of the shopping yourself."

Sarah made a face. "Does this mean she'll be doing the cooking as well? Do we have to put up with that *experimental* stuff?"

"Since when has spaghetti been experimental?" Joanne said, clipping Sarah lightly about the ear. "You'll eat what you're given and like it, you upstart." To her mother she said, "Take care while you're gone. I suppose you'll get there before dusk if you leave right away."

"Yes, I suppose so." Her mother was shaking her head, moist eyed, as she threw her arms first around Sarah, then around Joanne. "God, what a week. First Billy, now this. I really don't know what to think." For a moment Joanne felt her mother would never let go. Doubtless she'd have a good weep on the way, which would make her feel better. "We'll call you as soon as we're there. Are you sure you'll manage?"

"I'm sure."

But she couldn't confess her fears; or admit that she didn't relish the responsibility after what had taken place at the park. She saw them off from the gate with a wave and then stood at the kitchen window, staring out on Peterborough Lane long after the car had gone. Directly opposite, the lock-broken cemetery gate opened and closed and opened in a breeze that was getting up. No, she didn't relish the responsibility, but now that she had no choice, she'd defend Sarah and Jason with everything she had, her life if it came to that. If only she knew what it was she'd be defending them from.

"Isn't it dark in here?"

She started as Sarah, behind her, turned on the kitchen light on her way to the refrigerator. It was true: The hedge that David had pared down couldn't have been blocking the light after all, for the kitchen was gloomier than ever. The electric light helped a little, but it couldn't budge the vacuum cleaner's too-large shadow in its corner, or the darkened patch above the washing machine. The bulb was probably a sixty watt, when the kitchen really required a hundred.

"Where's Jason?" she asked sharply.

"In the other room, watching TV and wrecking the jigsaw puzzle I just put together for him. He's all right."

"I hope so."

"I only left him a minute ago."

"A minute can be a very long time." Joanne ran cold water into a glass, swilled, and refilled it. Then she didn't know what to do with it and poured out the water. "Promise me you won't let him out of your sight if I have to go out and leave you in charge."

Sarah turned from the refrigerator carrying a large tub of chocolate chip ice cream and placed it on the

108

counter beside the sink. "You know he's safe, Jo. Everything's made safe for him here."

"That's what I thought at the park today, how safe it all was, and look what happened."

"What *nearly* happened, you mean." Sarah studied her sister for a lingering second before prying the plastic lid from the ice cream with a spoon handle. "Are you sure *you're* all right, Jo?"

"Don't worry about me. I'm fine." But it sounded less than convincing, even to herself.

The light was fading, and by eight the streetlights were aglow. At half past, David phoned from Wolverhampton to say they'd arrived and that Mary was stable. With Jason safely bathed and bedded down, Joanne secured the baby gate at the top of the stairs and went to work on her bolognese sauce. When it was simmering, she put on the spaghetti, showered quickly, and ate with the plate on her lap in the living room. Sarah flipped back and forth through the TV channels with the remote, her share of the meal uneaten. And no wonder, since she'd been gorging herself on ice cream all day. The news was all bad, as always. Bombings abroad, murders at home; and she thought she had problems. Watching the items, one after another, she began to feel the way Hazel must feel: taking everyone else's burdens on board. Everything seemed to increase her fears—fears for Sarah and Jason, even herself. The crime rate statistics made her wonder if the house was secure enough.

That was why she remembered the doors were unlocked.

She moved through the house, sliding on bolts and chains, twisting keys in their locks. A window in the kitchen had been left open for ventilation while the spaghetti steamed away, and now she tugged it shut again. An army of moths patted and clung to the pane, even after she'd turned off the light.

By ten thirty, Sarah had fallen asleep on the couch. She hardly stirred when Joanne tried to coax her awake, and seconds later Joanne was carrying the sleeping bulk upstairs. She doesn't know me, Joanne thought, laying Sarah out on the bed, tugging the sheets to her chin. Nor does Jason. As long as they're asleep, I could be anyone, prowling through the house uninvited, entering this room or that one at will. Her thoughts were enough to startle her. She recalled the dream Sarah had related over breakfast one morning last week. Drawing the curtains together to close the gap, she hurried from the room.

It was rapidly becoming one of those nights. Here she was again, alert and unready for sleep, listening for the merest pin drop. She couldn't even read, since her thoughts were moving faster than the words. Instead, insanely, she settled down with the lights out to watch one of David's videos that she hadn't yet seen: *Dawn of the Dead*.

The film left her drained and wishing she had chosen something else, especially to follow the spaghetti bolognese. Worse, it only served to make her feel less secure than before. When the zombies broke into the supermarket, she felt it was her house they were invading. She had chosen the wrong night—the wrong week—to watch this, and thirty minutes from the end she stopped the tape.

Turning off the TV and leaving the living room, she hesitated before going to the stairs. Halfway along the hall, the door to the renovated basement stood half open, though she knew she had closed it earlier as part of her locking-up routine. Now, she found she needed to force the door with her body weight to close it: The latch was faulty, that was all; she couldn't have shut it properly the first time.

There was no way into the house through the basement, of course, and nothing down there except stereo equipment. It was just that the open door disturbed her. She couldn't imagine why. She knew only that for some reason it pricked her conscience, as though trying to remind her there was something she'd missed.

13

THERE WERE NO TWO WAYS ABOUT IT—the sooner she contacted Martin, the better. If anyone could explain what was happening to her, it was him.

Since the incident at the park yesterday—in fact, because of it—she had discovered two truths of equal importance: first, that the longer she stalled, avoiding Martin, the worse things became; second, that Sarah and Jason were also at risk. Whatever had seized Billy McGuire that night was just as liable to go after them too.

The only consolation, and it wasn't much of one, was that she was able, finally, to feel sorry for Billy. At least pity was better than nothing, and for so long nothing was all she'd been able to give him. But even this, her sadness on his behalf, was because he was no longer a threat. Dead, she could cope with him.

Alive, he had been a monster. Now the monster was buried, but her fear had not been laid to rest with him; now it was focused on other things: a mark like a handprint at the lakeside, a pale unformed shape flitting across a road. Something was about to give, she felt sure. She couldn't just wait for it to happen, doing nothing.

After breakfast she tried dialing Martin's number. She hoped she'd memorized it correctly—the sequence ended 007, like James Bond, she thought; or had it been 077? When no answer was forthcoming from the first, she tried the other, but that was not in service. Perhaps it was just as well, as she hadn't decided what to tell him if he asked where she'd got the number. As she hung up, she saw Sarah thumping downstairs, a mass of tangled hair and stretching arms straight from sleep. She was talking, but her yawn made nonsense of the words.

"I was saying that Jason's still out cold," she repeated, jumping the bottom three steps. "The fresh air yesterday must have knocked him for a loop."

"The longer he sleeps, the better," Joanne said. "Do you think you can hold the fort for a while? There are groceries to fetch, and an errand I have to run. I'll be a couple of hours at least."

Sarah shrugged. "Do I have any choice?"

"Not really."

"Then you'd better hurry up. And remember you owe me one."

"One what?" Joanne smiled, tugging on her faded denim jacket as she went to the door, where she halted, checking pockets for cash. "If he's restless, you can play your *Snowman* video. That's one of his favorites; it usually shuts him up for a while."

Sarah folded her arms indignantly. "I know what to do."

"Just remember what I told you. Don't let him out of your sight. And don't answer the door." She hesitated as something creaked in the hall, between the stairs and the kitchen. "And will you shut that damn basement door? If Jason gets on those steps—"

"You sound like Mom," Sarah said, and turned away. "I don't mind looking after him, it's the nagging that bugs me. Why don't you go now? Everything's fine."

Supermarkets had never rated among Joanne's favorite places. Years ago, at a local supermarket that was now a warehouse for carpets, she had received a bloody nose and concussion while bending to collect a jar of mayonnaise from a lower shelf. She had been shopping with her father, still several years from his death. As she straightened up, jar in hand, a boy rounded the corner too quickly, all elbows and knees. He might have been chasing someone, or being chased, for she remembered his laughter. They never saw each other: He was through and past her before she knew another thing, and down she went, her face alive with pain. She couldn't think of another reason why she should dislike shopping at supermarkets, so she had always put it down to that.

The nearest to home was the new Asda supermarket, formed like a city out of the landscape in the middle of nowhere. It stood, gray and foursquare, surrounded by parking lots, always busy, and beyond the parking lots countryside. It was on the 48 bus route between South Horton and Middleton, half a mile or so before the Westbury footpath. Nearer town the complex might have seemed to belong to something, but out here it looked unplanned, like an accident of nature; a monster that had formed itself out of nothing.

Today, the place reminded her of last night's film, not least because of the way the shoppers were plucking boxes and cans from the shelves. Not so much zombies as programmed machines on autopilot, she thought. They didn't seem to be looking at what they were buying. It was easy to imagine the shoppers being soldered together on production lines playing the same god-awful piped Muzak.

Half the girls Joanne had grown up and gone through school with were now working here. She recognized three of them at the checkouts as she pushed her cart through the turnstile toward the fresh vegetables. Of the fourteen checkouts only six were in use. Long lines were forming; children were beginning to cry.

115

Joanne pushed the cart along the first aisle, frowning at the labels. Usually this was her mother and David's weekly task, and she'd forgotten where everything was. Ah, the coffee and tea were on her right. If she'd made a list, she would have known whether she needed any. Farther along, soft drinks. A large bottle of Perrier, and for Sarah some lemonade. To her left were the oven-ready pizzas, which would save her the trouble of making one. She selected one topped with olives and tossed it into the cart.

At this rate she'd be laden by the time she was done; she'd never manage this weight as far as Martin's and would have to take it straight home instead. Shouldn't she have gone to Martin's first, leaving this until later? But she knew damn well she was stalling, putting the moment off. Martin wouldn't hurt her; he was on her side! Anyone seeing his face that night on the main street ought to know that. Furious with herself, she threw in croissants and a whole-grain loaf of bread for good measure.

A woman's distorted voice began announcing special offers as Joanne rounded the cart into the next aisle. Pasta shells, rice, whole-wheat spaghetti. Ahead, the checkouts were a shambles. A woman with a heaped-up basket was being turned away from a cash register where a sign in small print said, "Six items or less." Joanne saw the woman drop the basket and march away in despair. The lines at the other

116

registers were too much for her.

Another aisle. Pet foods on one side, cookies and breakfast cereals on the other. Several carts were jammed together halfway along the aisle, as if their owners had given up on them. Joanne was stooping low among the cookies, chocolate chip cookies in one hand, crackers in the other, when she heard a terrific crash to her right.

She stood up sharply, packages in hand. For a moment she was holding a jar of mayonnaise and she was back in the supermarket again, years ago, about to be knocked off her feet.

But no one was running at her. A fat woman twenty feet away had fallen and was sitting sprawled on the floor, a Sugar Puffs box clutched in front of her. There was a shocked and dazed expression on her face as the spilled contents of her hand basket rolled away in all directions—onions, cans of beans, a grapefruit. Past her, at the end of the aisle, a shadow flicked out of sight around the corner; several toothpaste boxes scattered to the floor as it went.

"Are you all right? Can I help?" Throwing in her crackers, Joanne abandoned the cart and set off toward the woman. "Did someone knock you over?"

The woman just sat there, speechless, clutching her cereal. She tried to speak, but nothing came. She waved a hand, pointing, mouth sagging open.

"Maybe I can help you to your feet," Joanne said, but the woman merely shook her head. Obviously she was too shocked to move. There was a crash in the next aisle and the sound of dumb, inane laughter. "Whoever did this to you," Joanne said, "they'll be dealt with if the security people get hold of them. Can I bring someone? Is there anything—"

Suddenly she stopped dead. Perhaps her own mouth sagged open, perhaps not, but she couldn't be sure of anything for several instants. Another crash had sounded, and another. With a world-weary sigh, the woman had dropped one arm down by her side. Astonished, Joanne stared at the Sugar Puffs carton. There was a gaping blank space on the front where Honey Monster ought to have been.

This was ridiculous! Imagination was one thing, insanity quite another. If she weren't careful, she'd be trading the former for the latter. Noise filled her head as she stood there, Muzak and beeping checkouts and the clatter of change; then more slow, hollow laughter from the aisle beside hers. She didn't pay the woman another second's attention.

Forgetting her groceries, she took off. She bumped against the last shelf as she rounded the corner, and more toothpastes went flying. Any minute now she would wake, she knew. She was dreaming bad dreams after sitting up late watching zombie films, that's what was happening. The shopping mall scenes had entered her subconscious and were now filtering through to her sleep. If she could only believe that—but this seemed as real as anything, as

118

real as the killing of Billy McGuire. So did the bottle of salad dressing she stepped on as she stumbled into the next aisle.

Her legs nearly went from under her. There was a stab of pain in her ankle as she threshed for balance. Then, as she straightened up, the market's clash of noise seemed to fade. The aisle she'd entered was a bomb site, the floor littered with spilled and smashed bottles and jars, a spreading pool of ketchup, a half-unfurled toilet roll. Why hadn't anyone come to attend to this? But the aisle was empty, of shoppers at least. At the far end, however, stood Honey Monster.

A man in a suit playing some ridiculous prank was her first impression. Who could feel threatened by this? He must have stood seven feet tall, baseball cap tweaked to one side, gelatine eyes as large as plates, a mouth like a grinning zip that might split his face into halves if he spoke. But there was no zip; bizarre as his appearance was, the glint in his eyes seemed all too real. She backed off as he took a leaden step forward.

"Joanne," he said.

Good God! He knew her name. The shock of hearing it on that awkward, dim-witted tongue turned her cold. In his left hand, more a fingerless paw than a hand in fact, he was clutching a jar of strawberry preserves. When he thrust it down, smashing it, she jumped. She tried speaking but could only manage a whisper.

"You're not for real," she gasped at him. "Are you?"

Down went another jar. "What do you think?"

"You must be a dream or a joke. Who told you my name? Who are you?"

"You ought to know who I am, Mommy."

"I'm not your mommy, you freak," she cried.

"I'm not a freak neither." He grinned.

Joanne picked up a bottle and hurled it. It shattered at Honey Monster's feet with a sound like a muffled bomb, stopping him short. Surely someone would come soon, hearing this. Where were the crowds of shoppers, thick as flies just a minute ago?

"Leave me alone," Joanne said, ketchup bottle at the ready.

But Honey Monster shrugged. "I can't."

"Why not? You're supposed to be friendly. Kids are supposed to love you. Why won't you stop this now?"

"Because I can't. Now that I'm here, I've got to wreak havoc. Don't ask me why, I just have to."

He was halfway down the aisle now, but his approach was dreamlike, in slow motion, and she didn't seem to be able to turn and run. Instead she let loose the ketchup bottle. It broke in Honey Monster's face, showering his shoulders and undersized T-shirt with redness. "Help!" she called out. "Here! Help! Here!" She flung another jar, another bottle.

The suddenness of the assault made her attacker

scream and turn tail. Not seeing where he was going, he blundered into a shelf on his right, skittling preserves and honey to the floor.

"I'll get you for this," he slurred over his shoulder. "You and the bastard who brought me here." With both huge yellow arms, he reached upward and hauled himself onto the shelves, began climbing toward the ceiling. The shelves rocked uncertainly under the weight. As an afterthought he tossed a couple of marmalade jars, which landed heavily without breaking.

"Who do you mean?" Joanne called after him. "Who *did* bring you here?"

"When I find him, I'll finish him," he seethed as though he hadn't heard her. "I'll pulverize him. I'll bite off his head, that's what I'll do. I'll make him pay for everything he's done."

Without another word, he flashed one hand violently at the ceiling, dislodging one of the tiles. A gap opened, square and just large enough for him to pull himself through. Not looking back, Honey Monster reached up into darkness and was gone.

Joanne stood alone amid the debris. Several men were approaching, twin guards in uniform and a man in a gray suit whom she took to be the manager. All were looking upon the scene with horrified eyes. "Just what in God's name is going *on* here?" the manager said, and one of the guards asked Joanne, "What do you think you're doing, miss?"

She was too dumbfounded to reply. Fortunately, the other guard saved her the trouble. "Up here," he said, staring at the hole where the tile had been. "Is this where they went?"

Joanne could only nod. When the manager took her arm, she realized how violently she was trembling. He led her away by the elbow and along the next aisle toward her cart. The fat woman had only just picked herself up and was now refilling her basket, item by item.

The manager made a sound in this throat. "Hell's teeth, what's been happening here? Did you get a good look at who did this? Could you identify or describe them?"

"I—" Joanne thought about it, then shook her head. "It was all so quick," she said feebly.

She couldn't face any more shopping. She would pay for what was in the cart and leave. At least the checkouts were less crowded than before, but everyone there seemed to be staring her way, as if she were something they'd never set eyes on before. If you'd seen what I've seen, she thought, you'd have found something worth staring at.

Joanne knew the girl on her checkout from school, but she didn't remember her name. The girl must have left at least a year ago. She smiled as Joanne piled foodstuffs onto the conveyor, and handed over two shopping bags, the bulge beneath her smock quite pronounced.

"Looks like you're well on your way," Joanne observed.

"This? Oh, yes, three months to go." She made a face at the pizza, turning it upside down to check the price. "What was the noise all about back there?"

"A couple of vandals breaking things," Joanne said. "I think they went out through the ceiling."

The girl shook her head. "You'd think with all the money they spend on security, nothing like that could happen."

Joanne nodded, but suddenly she felt less like talking. There was little doubt in her mind that Honey Monster, too, was connected to Martin Wisemann. For a moment there, it was as though she'd crossed over into his story "Cereal Killer." If nothing else, it proved how slyly unpredictable monsters were, appearing when and where they pleased.

Now the manager and his two young guards were running back and forth as if lost; all this supermarket security going to waste. Would even stricter security make any difference? She doubted it. She collected her change and, before she understood why, was running, bundling her shopping bags through the doors that slid open as she reached them.

She reached her stop ten minutes before the bus was due and could only stand there, shaking. If supermarket security couldn't keep out intruders, what hope were a few locks and bolts at home? She thought of the basement door, opening itself, and again heard its creak as she left this morning. How damn stupid could you get? She ran on toward the next stop, as if catching the bus from there would get her home sooner. She should never have left Sarah and Jason alone.

14

EVERY HORROR STORY HAD either a basement, a locked door, or a secret at its heart. Whatever it was Joanne had blundered into this week possessed all three. Staggering into Peterborough Lane, both shoulders aching from the groceries, she pictured the door in the hall standing open and the secret that had conjured itself up in the dark, while no one was looking, emerging. And the locked door? That was her own front door, facing the cemetery. Just now, she couldn't think of a more appropriate place to be.

Even when she'd knocked three times, no one answered. Where on earth were her keys? She knocked again and moved around to the kitchen window and tapped there, but could see nothing except empty counters. There were noises within, that was something, but what kind of noises? She might have been mistaken, but what she heard sounded uncommonly like a struggle taking place. God, if she could only find the quickest way in! She was turning from the window when a scream and a roar coincided indoors.

Whatever else happens, whoever else suffers, she thought, don't let it be Jason and Sarah! She must be to blame for all this, and if she only knew how, she might be able to help. Where were the cops when she *really* needed them? It was as if she'd wandered by chance into some idiot's made-up story; as if someone had plucked her from life, sketched scenes about her, surrounded her with terrors from dreams. It was all too much, expecting her to cope alone. She picked up a large smooth stone from the lawn and was about to put it through the kitchen window when she heard the front-door key being turned.

Sarah stood holding the door open. Her face dropped as soon as she saw Joanne. From the inside came another tortured scream, followed by a joyful whoop that Joanne knew instantly as Jason's. It seemed to take her an age, standing there foolishly, stone held at shoulder level, before she could think.

"Sarah, what the hell is going on here?"

Before Sarah could reply, Joanne dropped the weapon, pushing through the doorway and into the hall. Both bags of groceries lay forgotten on the step.

"You said not to open the door for anyone," Sarah was saying, following.

"For anyone *else*, I meant. What's this?"

She stood at the living room door in horror. It was almost as bad as she feared. When she'd retired last night, she had forgotten to remove *Dawn of the Dead* from the VCR, and here was Jason seated in front of the final few minutes, clapping his hands as blood and brains exploded in glorious color. "Look," he was screaming deliriously. "Look, look, look!"

In a rush of activity Joanne crossed the room, turned off the tape, planted herself defiantly in front of the screen, obscuring his view of white noise. To Sarah she said, "Why are you letting him watch that?"

Sarah shrugged. "He tore up *The Snowman*. He broke open the box and ate the tape. I couldn't find anything else to show him."

"Did you watch any of that yourself? Do you know what you were letting him see?"

"Sure. I thought it looked pretty good. Reminded me of your experimental cookery."

"I ought to give you a good hiding, I really ought."

"Why? What am I supposed to have done?" Sarah put her hands on her hips and stood there, indignant. "What's the matter with you anyway? I can't do anything right."

Joanne breathed out; the first time today she'd felt able to. Leaving the room, she laid a hand on Sarah's shoulder. "I'm sorry. You're right, you're doing just fine. It's just that I've got a lot on my mind."

127

Sarah nodded. "Billy, I guess."

"And one or two other things besides." But she didn't elaborate. She couldn't say what it was she most feared, couldn't begin to explain that the monster Sarah had described from her dream was most probably real. Instead she said brightly, "How would you like to bring in the shopping? I'll make it worth your while."

"How?"

"I brought pizza for your supper tonight."

"Uh-oh. Spare me that."

While Sarah brought in the groceries, Joanne returned to the phone and dialed: first 007, then 077. Still no answer and still not in service. She hadn't been meant to contact Martin. She slammed down the phone and went to the basement, where the door was firmly closed. Pulling it open, she flicked on the switch at the top of the steps.

Below, the basement was plushly silent, not at all the kind of place in which beasts roamed and drooled. She must have been mad to consider such a thing, but had she been mad at the supermarket? Even a short stint of normality was enough to make her question her judgment, and now she felt less convinced than ever.

In the kitchen she put away the shopping while Sarah unpacked. She removed the shrink wrap from the pizza, put the pizza on a plate on the table for later, then poured Perrier into a tumbler for herself.

"I'll be down in five minutes," she told Sarah before swinging a leg over the baby gate on the bottom step.

In the bathroom she undressed quickly and stood on the scales, arms at her sides, chest out, stomach in. Two pounds lighter this week without really trying. Presumably she had lost it through worry: some diet. Her reflection in the mirror above the sink hadn't changed, except that every muscle looked tight with tension. Having washed and dressed, she returned to the mirror with makeup. A touch here, a dab there, anything to get rid of the pale, haunted look. She took her time about it; soon she would be on her way to see Martin. Not that she was obliged to look her best for him, but she should at least try to be presentable. She was wondering whether to leave Sarah and Jason at Margaret's, give herself an easy mind at least on that score, when she heard the telephone ringing.

Before she was halfway downstairs, Sarah had lifted the receiver. "Hello? Hello?" she was saying. "Hello? Who is that?" There was a pause before she gazed up at Joanne. "For you, Jo. Someone called Martin."

Joanne was at the phone in an instant. From the living room came a sudden rush of TV noise—channels being changed, volume increasing—as Jason discovered the remote control. Covering the receiver, Joanne said to Sarah, "Take him into the kitchen and give him something to eat. I'll be there in a minute."

She waited until Jason had been coaxed away and the kitchen door closed before speaking. "Martin? Martin Wisemann?"

"That's right." The line crackled. "You must be the Joanne Towne I met at the bookshop."

"Yes, yes I am. I've been meaning to come over."

"And I've been expecting you. It's been a rather difficult week, I suppose."

"You could say that."

"Have you changed your plans, then? Do you still intend to see me?"

"As a matter of fact I'm planning to head over there now. If that's all right with you, I mean."

"The sooner the better," Martin said. "I'm calling, in fact, to urge you to come."

"Really? Why would you have to urge me?"

"It's better that we discuss it face to face. Before this thing goes any further."

"Before what thing—?" She faltered there. Did he in some way sense what she'd been going through? Did he *know*? "Martin, I don't understand . . ."

Again, the connection sputtered and faded. "I'd better not say more. There isn't much time. I want you to get yourself over here as quick as you can, and be careful." Something seemed to occur to him then, and briefly he fell silent. "Who answered the phone just now? Are there others there besides you?"

Jesus, what was he trying to tell her? "Yes," she began. "Yes, there are others." She sorely needed his help, and here he was making her more afraid than ever.

"Get them out," he said sharply. "I don't care where, but get them where you know they'll be safe. I can't explain now, just do as I say—"

He was about to continue when a scream drowned him out.

Joanne dropped the receiver as if it had scorched her. Like a light bulb in a detective film, it swung back and forth, Martin's voice small and thin on the end of it. "Hello? Joanne? Hello?"

As soon as the screaming began again, Joanne knew it was for real. It was Sarah, behind the closed kitchen door. The crash that followed sounded like a chair going over.

Every weird tale had its closed doors. They were part of the scenery, something the author threw in to conceal the forbidden, holding back secrets until the very last minute. Well, *she'd* had enough of that nonsense. Enough, God damn it, was enough! She ran to the kitchen, not thinking twice about what might be waiting there. All she knew—if she knew anything at all in that moment—was that nothing was impossible; that monsters could not be kept out, not by locks or bolts or by guardsmen in uniform; that the only course of action in the end was to stand and face the worst; that the greatest number of accidents happened at home.

If Billy McGuire's death had prepared her for the

worst, or Honey Monster's vandalism for the most fantastic, the most ridiculous, nothing had quite prepared her for this.

The first thing she saw when she burst in the kitchen was Sarah, mouth trembling agape, her arms around Jason as she dragged him from the table. A chair lay on its side. Next to it was Jason's bottle, half filled with milk and hastily dropped. On the table itself, something was moving.

There was perhaps a fraction of a second of total calm in Joanne's mind during which she felt her sanity leave her. If it ever returned, she didn't notice. Only madness, not even the wildest dreams, could explain the soft mass she saw dragging itself across the tabletop.

It was Pizza-Face—the artist's joke from above the fast-food stand in Arcadia, flat faced and many legged. At first glance it looked like a toad that had been squashed and topped with appetizers. Strands of melted cheese dripped from its edges as it hauled itself forward across the table. In the center of the bubbling, multicolored body, something like a mouth opened up; either side of it, bulbous eyes emerged with a plopping sound, olives like irises at their centers.

Sarah was almost in tears. "God, Jo, what *is* it?"

The reply was the merest whisper. "How should I know?"

But in a sense she *did* know. It was another idea from fiction, a seed once planted through reading that had now come fully alive, another horror invading her world uninvited.

"*Do* something!" Sarah screamed, yanking Jason toward the gap between the washing machine and the wall. "Why did you bring that into the house? Why can't you bring home *plain* food for once?"

The patches of darkness had vanished from the walls, but Joanne thought she knew where to. If the shadows contained power of some kind, that power was now being released in incredible ways. In the top drawer beside the sink were the kitchen knives, polished to sparkling. She pulled out the longest and sharpest, and swung back to face the pizza.

It had now reached the table's edge and, with a sucking noise, was rearing itself up on cheese and tomato stalk-limbs, ready to leap. The mouth between the unblinking eyes opened, and there was a sound like a gasp or a whimper that chilled Joanne to the bone. Perhaps the sound was Jason's or Sarah's. Whoever it was, she didn't care to hear more. Screaming, "Stay where you are!" at the others, she lunged forward, bringing down the knife.

Her timing couldn't have been better. She struck just as the pizza was launching itself. If she'd hesitated, she would have been done for. Everything happened at once then, but she thought she saw rows of jagged teeth in the mouth and a narrowing of the creature's eyes before she connected with the blade. The next thing she knew, there were splinters of wood flying upward and two halves of pizza sprawled on the tabletop, surrounded by flecks of tomato sauce. Across the kitchen Jason was beginning to cry painfully, heartbrokenly. She was about to turn and attend to him when the pizza halves began skittering off to opposite corners of the table.

God help her, now she'd created two for the price of one. Two new eyes plopped, two new mouths formed; there was more than enough melted cheese to go around. Unable to stop herself, Joanne brought the knife down again, chipping the table; and again for good measure. Suddenly there were four monsters, suddenly six. The smaller they became, the more revolting they seemed, yet she brought down the knife again and again, not thinking, no longer caring.

In the midst of her panic, it hadn't occurred to her that the smaller beasts were becoming more mobile. Lacking the bulk of their parents, they were able to jump clear of the table altogether. One sprang directly at Joanne, entangling itself in her hair. With a cry of disgust she tore it loose, thrust it down, and with her heel ground it out on the tiled floor. Three or four more were hopping away under the table. Several were headed toward the far side of the kitchen, where Sarah and Jason cowered.

134

"Jo! What . . . do . . . I . . . do now?" Sarah managed between sniffs and gasps. "Help me help me help me—"

Joanne dropped the knife. It had done nothing but multiply her problems. But what now? She looked breathlessly about for something that might help, but where to begin? This wasn't your everyday domestic situation.

Then her gaze fell on the vacuum cleaner, the hose and nozzle attachment still coiled about it. Well, why not? Anything was worth trying once. She dashed toward it, stamping on several of the creatures as she went, unwinding the electrical cord as quickly as she could manage. Her hands were shaking so badly, she fumbled as she fitted the plug to the nearest wall socket. As she looked across the kitchen, she saw numerous tiny monsters the size of grubs swarming from the table to the floor, careering up walls, dripping from the lamp shade.

"Sarah," she cried. "Get him out of here. Go to Margaret's. Keep him there until I come back for you."

"I don't think I can," Sarah said feebly. "I'm afraid. I can't move."

"*Move!*" Joanne yelled.

Sarah moved.

Steering Jason to his feet, she set off. As soon as they passed safely from the kitchen and the front door slammed, Joanne set the vacuum cleaner's suction control to "boost" and turned it on. Everywhere she looked, miniature bug eyes glowered, miniature mouths opened wide, drooling and sucking. She moved forward purposefully, passing the nozzle this way and that across the tiles and walls, easing it into alcoves and corners.

The beasts offered little resistance. In less than a minute she had almost cleared them from the kitchen. One clung to a table leg for a second, then was gone. Another scrambled toward an open cabinet beneath the sink, but to no avail. They might have been quick and relatively agile, but they hadn't the strength to fight. Perhaps they weren't really a threat—she couldn't imagine what damage a *pizza* might do, for God's sake—but she wasn't prepared to take chances. She couldn't afford to take anything lightly. Switching off the Hoover, she turned ready to pack it away, and immediately went sprawling headlong over the cord.

Somehow, in falling, she'd managed to knot herself up in the cord. How useless she sometimes was! She grappled to free herself, fingers working the loop that constricted her ankle. As she did so, she heard what sounded like the harsh push and pull of breathing nearby. It didn't take her long to locate it, for the Hoover's dust bag was expanding and contracting like an artificial lung.

It was then that she knew she hadn't just tripped. She hadn't even put an end to the threat; all she'd done was transfer it elsewhere, given the monster the chance to become something else. Now, like a thing possessed, the Hoover was beginning to rock itself back and forth, back and forth, while the bag was expanded further, pressurized from within. Whatever was inside it was rapidly growing, readying itself to break out.

She didn't want to be here when it did. She tried to sit upright, at the same time tearing at the cable that held her leg and that seemed to be pulling tighter. Beside her, the Hoover flung itself haphazardly into the table, and another chair went noisily over. She was sobbing with rage and frustration, but the sounds seemed outside her, like someone else's. She happened to look up from her task in the same instant the plug freed itself from its socket and came whistling toward her.

Before she knew it, the plug had wrapped itself twice around her other leg, binding both ankles together. Joanne cried out, but who would hear, let alone rush to help? To her horror she felt herself being dragged, slowly, across the tiled floor. Above her, dust and fluff billowed upward as something buffeted the Hoover's dust bag from within.

Incredibly, she was aware only of how bright it seemed in here, how many dark patches had deserted the kitchen. There was a crash as the vacuum cleaner slammed itself sideways into a wall; a wheezing as something tried vainly to break out. She didn't dare even look at it now. There was only one slender hope, and if she couldn't turn hope into action soon, there'd be no telling what would come next. Sobbing with fear as well as with rage, she groped, left arm at full stretch, for the knife she had dropped.

It was just out of reach. Her fingernails brushed it, then the cable yanked at her feet and the knife spun slightly away from her. Whatever it was that held her, whatever power, there was no doubt it meant business. The pizza had been nothing by comparison: By drawing it into the vacuum, she'd done it a favor. If it ever got beyond this room and outdoors, she thought— But she mustn't allow that to happen. Summoning the last of her strength, she lunged to her side, grasping for the knife.

This time she had it, though she clutched the blade, which dug into her fingers. Transferring it to her good hand, her right, she began to slice at the cord, first through the insulation, then the three color-coded wires, the stubborn stranded copper at their centers. Seconds later she was free, the connection between the Hoover and herself neatly severed.

Joanne took to her feet; the cord fell lifelessly from her. Stepping clear of the sagging coiled wire, she rounded the Hoover slowly, keeping her distance. The hose and nozzle reared up like a charmed cobra as she passed; she brandished the knife, returning the threat. A silence ensued. Her vision was blurring, her heart racing; everything seemed such a whir and confusion. Dust from the Hoover bag fogged the air, thick enough to taste. Momentarily, everything seemed to have stopped, waiting, as she neared the doorway, backing clear of danger. But would she ever be truly clear of danger? After today she doubted it. Behind her she heard the door to the basement creaking open again.

Then she turned and fled into the hall, meaning to continue on through the front door and beyond to safety. It was as she set off that the beast came to life again. She heard it blundering through the kitchen, heard the tearing of the dust bag as something tried to emerge, smelled the grime and filth in the air as it gained on her, coughing up dust.

Turning right past the stairs, she saw the telephone still hanging and swinging, forgotten. Martin must wonder what the *hell* was going on here. Well, there was no time to explain. She wouldn't have time for anything if she didn't act soon. What difference would if make if she did flee outdoors and away toward far-distant streets? Would she ever be truly free? Of course not; she knew that now. If she managed to escape this demon, there would always be others, watching and waiting to catch her. Sooner or later she'd have no alternative but to stand and fight, to do what she could. Reaching the basement door, she put on the brakes, swinging around to meet her pursuer.

The Hoover trundled straight toward her, not

stopping, hose and nozzle trailing behind. Smoke rose from a tear in the dust bag and for an instant she thought she caught sight of a face inside: a many-eyed face made of putty or jelly. She didn't wait to look closer. Bracing herself, she seized the Hoover with both hands, helping it through the open door and over the first of the basement steps.

Gravity did the rest. There were twelve uncovered stone steps leading down. The vacuum cleaner took them all at once, and she heard the smash at the bottom as she pushed shut the door, leaning her weight against it. For a time, in the hush that followed, she wondered whether she'd ever be able to move from the door. Days from now her mother and David would return to find her here, still forcing the door closed, ensuring that nothing came out. She stood, scarcely breathing, wondering whether she dared turn and go. Then she heard movement down below, as if something were picking itself from the floor. Even then, she didn't make herself shift until she heard footfalls coming up the steps.

The fall had done nothing but release what had grown in the Hoover. Its bulk rocked the door from the other side as Joanne stumbled backward away from it. Maybe the thing in the basement had no hands, which was why it was battering the door instead of simply turning the knob.

But she didn't care to find out. Hardly aware she was doing so, she picked up the still-swinging

140

telephone and said, "Martin? Martin? What do I do *now*?"

There was no answer, though. The connection had been cut, or he'd finally given up on her. All she could hear was static, though at first she had thought it was breathing. She wouldn't have been surprised if it had been that. She doubted that anything could surprise her now.

Along the hall, the basement door thundered. What was she trying to prove, still here, still clutching the phone? The sooner she got out, the better. Should she head straight to Martin's? There was a chill in the air as she replaced the receiver, a scent of cut grass and freshly dug earth issuing in on the wind. But the house was supposed to be secure, everything firmly shut. She turned from the telephone to see the front door standing wide open.

And at the threshold, fresh from the grave, the grinning figure of Billy McGuire.

15

"WE'VE UNFINISHED BUSINESS," he said.

It was the last thing she wanted to hear.

If there had been any fight left in her, it deserted her then. There was nothing more she could do; the weird tales had swallowed her whole. She fell sideways against the wall, doing her best to keep her feet. Whatever happened now, she mustn't faint or fall, mustn't make herself vulnerable.

In a voice she hardly recognized, she said, "Why, Billy? Why?"

"Because," he said, but nothing more. He stepped closer, through the doorway and into the hall.

It was coming up for air, she thought, remembering a line from a story; a story in which something had groped its way out of the ground. She had read it, dreamed it, and now was living it. The story was one of Martin's, but then it would have to be, wouldn't it? It seemed such a tidy detail of plotting, another segment of a jigsaw puzzle fitting neatly into place. She even remembered the title: "Lover Come Back." Then she began to laugh, or perhaps weep. She'd reached the point where she couldn't tell one from the other.

Billy said, "No one, I mean *no one* treats me the way you did and gets away with it. Did you think you were off the hook just because of what happened to me?"

She had thought she stood a better-than-even chance. "But you're dead," she said. "You're dead and buried. Doesn't that mean anything to you?"

"It means a lot. But it doesn't mean forgiveness." Mud caked from head to foot, each step scuffing earth across the carpet, Billy advanced. In a voice thick with soil, he said, "Jealousy's a powerful thing, you know. More powerful than you or me, or even the grave. Strong enough to bring me back."

Joanne shook her head in sheer disbelief. Away to her left, the basement door sighed from another assault. "But Billy, there was nothing to be jealous *about*. The problem was you just wouldn't trust me, you wouldn't believe me when I told you the truth."

"Since when did you tell me the truth, Jo?"

"There you go again. How long do you think I could let you go on accusing me? I have feelings too. I never—"

"You killed me," he said, spitting out soil, wiping one filthy hand backward across his chops. "You took away everything I had and then led me to my death."

"That's not the truth and you know it. You were killed because you were jealous and wanted revenge. You thought—"

"I know what I thought."

"Well, you were *wrong*, Billy, totally wrong. I never had anything to do with Tim Lockwood."

"I know that now." He halted for a moment; an earthworm pushed into view between the buttons of his burial shirt. "Yes, I realize he wasn't the one; that bastard, the writer, it was him all along. Don't tell me that isn't so!"

God help her, he was worse than before. Not only dead but deranged. What did it take to convince him? And to think she'd pitied him after the funeral!

Behind her, a wordless shout went up in the basement, a sound neither human nor animal. It hung in the hallway for an age before fading. Billy McGuire didn't so much as flinch. Perhaps where he came from the sound was quite common. Perhaps he was too preoccupied to notice. As he flung himself toward her, arms outreaching, she saw madness glint in his eye and knew all too well why he'd come. He intended her to go to the grave with him; he wouldn't rest until he possessed her completely.

At least, thank goodness, the thickness of mud

slowed him down. She was able to throw herself clear of his lunge. He struck the wall near the phone as she rolled to her left. Soil fell from his clothing in thick, moist lumps. She turned toward the front door just as the breeze pulled it shut.

The shock of seeing that caused her, briefly, to lapse. Billy's clawed hand raked her shoulder, tearing the skin as well as her blouse. Crying out, she stumbled away from him. The front door would take her two or three seconds to open; much longer than she knew she could spare. Instead she turned to her left, vaulting the baby gate, hastening upstairs.

She ought to have known better. From here there was no way out unless she smashed a window and jumped, probably to her death. Then she'd be exactly where he wanted; she'd never be able to avoid him again. She reached the top step, running headlong toward the bathroom, the only upstairs door that would lock. She didn't glance back, but despite her own ragged breath she could hear him struggling at the baby gate, then thumping heavily up the stairs. He reached the top as she entered the bathroom, slammed the door, slid the bolt into place. A split second later the thing that had once been Billy hit the door from outside, punching and kicking, then working the knob to and fro. At least he had more sense than the one in the basement; he knew what the knob was for.

Finally he threw a couple more halfhearted

punches at the woodwork and said, "You'll open this door if you know what's good for you."

"You must be joking," Joanne said. "As soon as this door is open, you'll kill me."

"Only because I love you. I want us to be together always."

That wasn't even worth a reply. Had it ever crossed his mind that *she* might want otherwise? Turning, she looked helplessly about her, wondering what she could use against him. Razor blades, possibly? But David used an electric shaver. Her mother's hair spray then—she might aim it into his face as she swung wide the door, but how could she be sure it would work? The situation was new to her, she couldn't exactly draw on her past experiences, she could only—

She stopped there, wondering. No, she couldn't relate any of this to experience; only to things she had read.

Wait, now wait. She needed to think, if her head would stop buzzing. An idea was trying to take shape for her. Somewhere in the chaos there must be a pattern, a detail she'd overlooked. She was dealing with monsters from fiction, that much she knew. Even though the creature outside had taken Billy's appearance, it might as well have been anyone, since he was doing exactly as the boyfriend from hell in the story had done.

"You'd better let me in. I'm getting impatient," the voice beyond the bathroom door was telling her.

She tried to ignore it, tried to think clearly. Not *everyone* in the stories had perished, of course. Many had been eaten, torn apart, left heaped up like so much raw meat. But some had won out; some had discovered the light at the end, had slain their dragons, had staked their vampires. In "Lover Come Back," how had the heroine dealt with the threat?

She was almost certain the girl had survived. Had she climbed from a window? Perhaps it was worth risking the fall.

Joanne pulled up the sash and looked out. The bathroom was directly above the kitchen and faced onto Peterborough Lane. Across the street the cemetery gates were wide open; convenient for Billy's comings and goings. But from here it looked like there was no way out; no ledges to cling to, and the sheerest drop to the concrete below. She doubted she'd be able to propel herself as far as the lawn, and in any case she'd be liable to break her neck if she tried.

Behind her, Billy was renewing his assault on the door. So much for Martin's story: The girl had probably leaped to safety, landed well, and gone on to fight another day. Joanne couldn't expect the same good fortune. Fiction might be ruling her life, but she was still forced to deal with real pain, real loss, real consequences. If she could only maneuver her way past Billy, there might be a hope. To her left a car moved slowly and loudly along the street. She heard it before she saw it, the exhaust backfiring. Even if she found her voice, the driver would never hear her. This was all so *unfair*, God damn it!

But now the car was pulling over, creeping along the curb as though checking the house numbers. Outside Joanne's gate, it stopped. She buried her knuckle in her mouth, afraid to believe her eyes. The vehicle was a green VW, and Martin Wisemann was climbing out.

It was as if someone had written a savior into her darkest scene. Before he laid a hand on the gate, she had pushed up the sash as far as it went and was waving, screaming his name.

Martin looked up. He came slowly up the drive, watching her. Something he was carrying glinted cold and metallic at his side.

"What was going on when I called? I thought you were coming over. I thought I heard something—"

"It's still going on!" Her voice sounded shrill with panic. The door rocked behind her again. "There's something trying to break into this room. And there's something in the basement. Help me, Martin, for God's sake be careful but help me."

Martin nodded; he showed little emotion and seemed not to need further explanation. He was wearing a loose-fitting combat jacket, and as he turned his attention from Joanne to the house, she realized how appropriate that was, as if he'd come here fully prepared for war. Well, he wasn't about to

148

be disappointed. He darted out of sight below her and then she heard the front door being forced.

She needed to meet him at least halfway. She shouldn't expect him to do everything. Collecting her mother's hair spray from the windowsill, she went back to the door. Then she waited for the sound of Martin coming inside before she slid back the bolt, turned the knob, and stepped out into the path of Billy McGuire.

He'd probably heard her calling to Martin and guessed her plan, for when he saw her, he didn't so much as hesitate. As soon as the bathroom door swept ajar, he came at her with both earth-dusted hands. Joanne aimed the hair spray vaguely toward his face and let rip.

Nothing happened. The cannister was used and empty, should have been thrown out months ago. She flung it at Billy as he careered through the doorway, slamming her into the tiled wall beside the washbasin.

When she tore at his arms to free herself, the shirt sleeves parted like butter. For a moment she thought she heard Martin's footsteps on the stairs; then again, that was probably her heart in her mouth.

Why was he taking so long, though? Probably it had been only a second since the front door had slammed open. She was dragging for breath, for air that tasted of dampness and earth as Billy pressed his face toward hers. There was murder in his eyes, and he seemed to have run out of conversation at last, but there was nothing he could say now to surprise her. She threw herself violently to the left, but Billy came with her, still gripping her arms. As they tumbled from the bathroom and onto the landing together, she clawed at his face, bringing fingerloads of soil down from his scalp and into his eyes.

It was enough to shake him off, at least enough to loosen his grip. While he groped at his blinded eyes, she ducked away into the path of Martin Wisemann. For an instant it was like gazing into a mirror: In Martin's face she saw her own deepest fears and, as his gaze went to Billy, her own revulsion.

"Good God, it's worse than I thought," he said under his breath. Then, steadying in both hands the jack handle he'd brought from the car, he said to Joanne, "Get moving!"

She hesitated, perhaps too startled to act. When Martin pushed her toward the stairs, she found her legs wouldn't stop. Taking the steps two at a time, she reached the foot of the stairs too quickly, went sprawling over the baby gate. As she picked herself up, she heard Billy upstairs, screaming with rage; then the thick damp sound of the jack handle colliding with Billy, two, three times, after which everything stopped.

For a time the house seemed more silent than a church, but there was nothing remotely holy about it. Then she heard Martin, his words just audible above the sudden thunder of feet on the upstairs floorboards: "Jesus, I ought to have known! How could I be so—?"

The rest was cut off to her, partly because whatever she'd locked in the basement had renewed its attack on the door. She was backing away from the stairs when she saw Martin racing down toward her, mud-caked weapon in hand, mouth open. Behind him came Billy McGuire, hands outstretched, teeth bared like a dog's. It was then that Joanne remembered the outcome of Martin's story "Lover Come Back," and realized she'd forgotten the whole point of it. Because he was already dead, the one thing the boyfriend from hell could never do was die. His rage—and his jealousy—would go on forever. Yes, the girlfriend had escaped, but only until the next time, or the time after that.

"Get yourself to the car!" Martin yelled.

Hurdling the gate, he half pushed, half dragged her with him, through the door and along the drive, between the gateposts at the end and into the car. No birds trilled in the open air; no dogs barked in distant streets. Once she'd collapsed in the passenger seat, Joanne looked back at the house, breathing hard. The open entrance gave a clear view of an empty hallway, no sign of Billy, or of anything else. Though she must have been mistaken, she thought she saw the basement door sighing outward of its own accord, then coming to rest about two thirds

151

ajar. Nothing came out—or it if did, it must have been after Martin leaned across her and tossed the jack handle into the back, next to the newspaper's headline, LOCAL MURDER SHOCK. Returning to the wheel, he accelerated the VW along Peterborough Lane.

16

FIFTY YARDS ALONG, he went into a road turn, pulling the Volkswagen around in a sharp U that caused the tires to screech before heading back the way he had come. Joanne watched first her own house, then Margaret's, go sailing by, and thought, Please take care of them, don't let anything harm them.

At the first opportunity she would call Margaret, make sure she would keep Sarah and Jason there. She would make the call brief, pretend she was in a hurry, and hence avoid having to explain. How could she make Margaret understand what she didn't understand for herself?

While Martin drove along Fairview Road, she pulled on her seat belt and stared, unseeing, from the window. After a while Martin took out a pack of cigarettes, rolled down the window on his side, and smoked. Joanne rolled down her own window, so that the wind could rush into her face. Nothing was said, even when the silence between them grew painful to the point of her wanting to smash it. For the present at least, horror had killed all conversation.

Soon they were on the outskirts of South Horton and she was ticking off landmarks—The Three Horseshoes pub, the Don, the beginnings of open country. They all seemed like details in a story to her now, no more real than anything else. Now and again Martin flicked his cigarette at the dashboard ashtray, and she remembered the mounds of butts in his room at the cottage. The Asda turnoff came and went, as did the one for Westbury.

Joanne said, "Aren't you supposed to be turning there?"

"We will be," he said, "but later. There's something we have to take care of in town first."

"We?"

He looked at her, heavy eyed. "We're both involved. You ought to have gathered that much by now."

"I have, I suppose. But involved in *what*?"

Turning to face the road again, he put out his cigarette in the ashtray, and she saw that his hand was shaking.

They parked, ten minutes later, in the side street

where she had seen him last. She remembered how preoccupied he had been at the time, how remote. If anything, he was now even worse. Today, he had an undernourished, unshaven look that Joanne had always associated with derelicts. But his weary eyes, the lines on his face, told the truth; and if she had thought more closely about it, it was the same truth she'd seen when she'd first caught sight of him, at the scene of the crash near Arcadia.

"Do you want to stay here or come with me?" he said when he'd finished maneuvering the car.

She followed at a jog to keep up as he walked, head down, to the main street. They stood side by side at the crosswalk, not talking, while traffic blurred by, riffling her hair and raising the taste of exhaust fumes far back in her throat. It was hard to imagine almost a week had passed since she'd been here; a week overflowing with horrors that, at times, she felt sure she'd dreamed up. But she'd dreamed and imagined nothing—otherwise, what was she doing here with Martin? On both sides of the street she saw lovers laughing, arm in arm in the lowering sun. It seemed so unjust, the way they were coasting through life while she . . . But the traffic was slowing for the lights, and Martin was ushering her into the street, toward the pedestrian mall.

She guessed, wrongly, that he was about to show her where the pale figure had vanished that night. It was about here, among the benches and saplings planted into the asphalt, that Joanne had lost sight of it. Two rows of shops like anonymous doors in a high-rise stood facing each other. Halfway along on the right was a drugstore, which reminded her she ought to get something for an oncoming headache. Behind her eyes, a pulse was beginning.

Instead of taking her to the shops, though, Martin dodged left, through the swinging front doors of the library. She followed him in, past the counter where a bored young assistant checked in and checked out books with an electric light pen, past the notice board with its outdated posters for last month's arts fair, through another set of double doors to the library itself.

Joanne had always much preferred the old building in South Horton, with its antiquated furnishings and musty smells like the upstairs room at Carleton's Booksellers. The new site, like everything else in the main town, was larger, better equipped, and quite dead. It was in every way modern, with tubular steel shelves and huge smoked-glass windows on all sides and always, in the background, the electronic *bip* of bar codes being read. A stairwell at the far end led upstairs to the children's library, two reading rooms, and a study area. It was toward the stairs that Martin was leading her.

At the bottom he said, "Wait here. I'll be down in a minute."

She browsed at random while he was gone, picking

156

out and putting back books whose titles didn't register with her at all. She couldn't even be sure which section this was. Near the exit an old man had fallen asleep on a chair, his whole body slowly tilting to one side. Eventually Martin came up beside her, pushing a book into her hands.

"Here, take care of this for a minute."

It was an illustrated copy of *The Pied Piper of Hamelin*; she looked at it, then at Martin, vacant eyed. "I hope you're planning to explain what you're doing," she told him, but Martin was already rushing toward the free-standing shelves of novels. Frowning, still balancing the book like a tray between her hands, she came with him, along the section marked A–D, quickly past E–H, then on from there.

Martin wasn't a browser. He seemed to know exactly what he was looking for. She was not especially surprised when he drew up short at W, seizing three novels of his own. He stood for a moment longer, running his forefinger over the spines on the shelf. Satisfied that none of his books had strayed under different letters, he tucked the three under his arm and smiled timidly at Joanne.

At the counter, after the double doors, he slapped down his driver's license and stood fidgeting while the girl filled in a membership form. His coded ticket would take a month to come through, she explained. Meanwhile, if he wanted these books, there would be a small charge. He waited for the *bips* while their bar codes were read, then pushed a five-pound note toward her. Not waiting for change, he swept up the books from the counter and marched out.

Before they reached the main street, Joanne remembered her headache. She had already twisted the cap from a bottle of aspirin by the time she emerged from the drugstore, dry swallowing two on the way to the car. Martin hadn't waited for her, and was sitting behind the Volkswagen's wheel when she got there. He had placed the books on the dashboard in front of the passenger seat and was sitting quietly, oblivious of her, as though trying to reach a vital decision. Finally he sighed and took out another cigarette and flipped it between his lips. "These," he said, gesturing at the books, "are the last. I'm sure of it."

Then he turned the ignition key and sat there, revving the engine. "Did you ever read that before?" he said, indicating *The Pied Piper of Hamelin*. "I think you should take another look at it."

Suddenly Joanne had had enough. She spoke as quietly as she could, scarcely containing her anger. "Do you mind telling me what you're supposed to be doing? You said we were *both* involved, but I'm starting to feel like something you brought along for the ride." She crossed her arms on her chest to show how immovable she was. "So far, what I've seen I couldn't begin to describe. If I told it to the police, they wouldn't believe me. They wouldn't believe that every day is becoming another damn chapter from one of your books. They're searching for clues, but in all the wrong places; they're looking for Billy McGuire's killer, but you and I know they'll never come close to finding him. But Martin, if I can't talk to you, there's no one at all, there's nowhere for me to go. Will you please tell me what it is I'm caught up in?"

Martin looked at her, so unblinkingly that for a moment she felt herself blushing. She closed her eyes, pressing a thumb and a forefinger to the bridge of her nose. Despite the tablets, her head was beginning to throb like a factory.

When she opened her eyes again, Martin was pulling out into traffic. "You're right," he told her. "You deserve an explanation. But please don't expect a solution." At the first junction the turn signal ticked patiently while he waited for a gap. "I would've contacted you sooner or later to discuss this, Joanne. But I had to be sure."

"Had to be sure of what?"

"That it was you I'd been looking for."

For a second she thought she'd misheard him. "Let me get this straight. *You* were looking for *me*?"

He gave a nod. "When we first met, last week, I sensed there was something between us. But I had to be sure. It was all too convenient, the way we bumped into each other. After I left you, I decided to call you later that day, but when I did you were out. The next thing I knew, there was an item in the papers, the killing of Billy McGuire, and your name was mentioned; you were among the ones who saw him last. The connection was just begging to be made. It was *Nightstalk*, you probably realized that. I waited to see if you'd come to the house as we'd planned, but you didn't—and then I began to be afraid. I began to think you had—" He paused, slowing as they approached the main town traffic circle. "Well, it's a good thing I *did* begin to worry; otherwise you'd still be locked in that upstairs room."

"That's all very well," Joanne said, "but you're making it sound as if you knew in advance that this would happen. You were looking for me even before you knew I existed."

"Yes." He glanced at her, then back at the road. "And you were looking for me."

"I was?"

"In a sense, you were, yes. You were searching, let's say, for something different; something to grab you and lift you out of your drab little life. It just so happened that you chose me and my stories to do it—I was the high you were after. Billy McGuire was a part of the life you were trying to escape."

"Supposing that's true." She was rolling up the window at her side to quiet the thunder of air. "How could you know so much about me? We never met;

160

as far as you're concerned, I'm just some bimbo who reads your books."

"No," he said, "that isn't how it is. I know you because I am *like* you. Why else did you think I wrote that stuff? Why do you think I still do it, even though no one reads it these days? I do it because I need to, because it's my own private high. It's a madness that has to be let loose from its cage now and then. That's how I know how you feel. Besides," he added as an afterthought, and took a deep breath before finishing, "this isn't the first time. What we're going through now has happened before."

She felt she was close to uncovering a secret that was best left concealed. As the outskirts of town gave way to the country, she asked, "Where, and when?"

"The circumstances don't matter. What matters is that I came here fully expecting an end to it all. I'd hoped that by making a fresh start, I'd be safe, that everyone else would be safe."

Joanne was biting her knuckle so hard, she wanted to cry out for the pain. "Martin, are you telling me you caused this? You *made* those horrors come crawling out of the woodwork? Is that what you're saying?"

She wished she hadn't asked. She wished she were able to close her eyes and open them again and be free of the sordid nightmare forever. But Martin was nodding almost imperceptibly, and slowing the car while he looked at her. "Yes," he said, "yes, I am responsible for this. But, Joanne, there's something you're going to have to know sooner or later: So are you."

17

SUDDENLY AND WITHOUT WARNING the land was gone from under the car. The VW nose-dived into space, seeming to hang there for a second, and was then careering down the incline toward Westbury. Even though Martin was riding the brake, the slope threw them forward so sharply, the seat belts locked. At the bottom, the VW jogged through a shallow stream and slithered slightly on the mud at the far side, and then they were turning in through the gates outside Martin's house. Joanne put a hand to her mouth as the full extent of the house and its grounds came into view.

She'd thought she'd grown immune to shock—numbed to the bone by everything she had seen and heard since Honey Monster's appearance at the supermarket. Perhaps the first thing she noticed was the smell: the ripeness on the air like a rottenness of fruit, like the hint of something fragrant that had turned. The building itself looked unchanged—even the boards were in place at the upstairs windows—but the whole of the lawn, as far as the sweeping gravel drive, was transformed. A bluish-gray fungus, or something very like fungus, had stolen across it, stranding the table and chairs in the center. It seemed to have smothered the grass entirely, except for the odd greenish tuft here and there. Lumps of the stuff had grown up like toadstools as tall as men, or like stalagmites with white dripping peaks.

When Joanne let her hand fall slackly to her side, Martin said, "I know. It's been coming to this for days."

He parked near the front of the cottage and rounded the VW to open the door for Joanne while she sat, staring out in disbelief. Something that might have been an apple or a lump of fungus dropped from a tree across the lawn. Gray slime coated one outer wall of the summerhouse; some had found its way inside. Even the hedgerows were flecked with it.

"What is this?" she asked as Martin led her around to the back, where more of the blue-grayness predominated.

"It's a sign," Martin said, "that whatever's taking place is near to being finished." He said no more, but she thought she was beginning to understand. Having budged open the locked kitchen door, he led her inside and through the hall, stopping outside the living room. "In here," he said.

She glanced once up the stairs—the door at the top was still closed, but silent—and then she went in.

The room was just as she remembered, except for the ash-clogged fire that was trying to burn in the grate. There was a faint smell of damp logs and scorched paper, and above that the stale hum of old cigarettes. The large front window looked out on a blue-gray-fungus world, giving her the impression that everything out there was like that. Perhaps, soon, it would be.

"Please," Martin said, "sit down and be comfortable. You need to rest."

Joanne took the larger of the two chairs in front of the fire, drawing her feet in their soft white canvas shoes underneath her. Looking at the photograph on the mantel, she said, "Your wife?"

"My wife." He nodded; and briefly, he was transported, forgetting himself. Then he went and opened a cupboard beneath one of the bookshelves, began pouring brandy into two tall tumblers. "The glasses aren't the right sort, I'm afraid, but drink this. You'll need it."

She sipped at the drink and winced. Something cracked and sparked on the fire, but there was nothing romantic about the scene. Presently she felt something loosen in her chest, as if the brandy were uncoiling tension. Then she realized how exhausted she was; how loudly her body was calling for sleep.

Martin stood above her for a minute, his eyes on the photo of his wife. He had placed the library books on the mantel beside her. Nodding in silent agreement with whatever he was thinking, he came and sat opposite Joanne.

"She," he said, "was the start of all this. If you're going to understand anything, you should know about her. We'd been married four, four and a half years when I lost her. I'd been writing full-time during most of those years, and I know I would never have coped without her support. Maybe if she hadn't given me such encouragement, she might be alive today. I'd still be leaving my stories unfinished, or screwed up and thrown in the trash. But Josie—her name was Josie—turned me into a writer. She was my prize, the thing I loved more than anything. I was so much in love, I lived in daily fear of anything happening to her, of losing her.

"I tried to deal with that fear in a story. You wouldn't have read it, it was the first of my unpublished writings. You see, Joanne, I've always thought I should try to set down my deepest fears on the page; it's the only way I have of dealing with them, making them public, saying Yes, I can handle this now." He paused to stare into the ailing fire, then into the depths of his glass. "What I did was, I tried to put Josie at the heart of a story; I thought that if my heroine died—I always fall in love with my heroines—it would be a way to acknowledge my

166

feelings for Josie. Of course, I couldn't have told that to *her*. And I'd swear that when she read the finished thing, she didn't even recognize herself. But eventually, the tale was told, I'd got it out of my system. I'd purged myself of the fear.

"I *thought*."

There was a moment then, a lull, where Joanne could see he didn't want to go on and couldn't bring herself to ask the question that would make him. She swallowed brandy and waited. Her tongue felt singed and enlarged, her eyes on the verge of uncontrollable tears.

At last Martin said, "The next thing I knew, she was dead. I won't go into the details, but I lost her in exactly the same way that I lost the girl in my story. There was an accident: no question about that. It wasn't the sort of happening that caused an enquiry. The police came and went, arrangements were made, everything happened in slow time, it was all cut and dried. But *I* knew, you see, that I'd killed her. Somewhere between me writing it and Josie reading it—" He stopped and looked sharply at Joanne. "Are you beginning to see now? Does it make more sense to you?"

She wanted it not to, but yes, even with the brandy beginning to cloud her senses, something was becoming clear. "But it was only a story," she managed, her tongue feeling slow to the point of being tied. "It was only something you made up."

Martin shook his head. As yet, he hadn't so much as sniffed at his own drink. Now he downed it in one. "Is that what you feel when you tuck yourself in with a good book? When you begin, slowly, to lose yourself; and then, the next day, you can't concentrate on anything you're supposed to be doing because you need to get back to this world you've entered? Do you feel it's only a story then?"

"No," Joanne said truthfully. "No, I don't."

"They might be just words on a page to some," he was saying, "but you and I know there's more to it than that. And we know that we're in it together; when you read what I've written, we're a team, we're conspiring against the world, we're escaping together toward lands we'd both rather live in, where we're able to deal with whatever comes at us. And somewhere between my sitting at that desk and your sliding into bed between the sheets with the words, somewhere along the line . . . something happens to make the people on the page come alive and be real."

She nodded, if only to urge Martin on.

"It's much like the point I always reach in a story where the characters I thought I'd dreamed up start doing their own thing. Suddenly it's as if they're saying No, I can't do that; No, I wouldn't be caught dead doing anything like that; or Wouldn't it be better if I did this instead of this? And then I cry out with frustration and joy because I know they're alive, so much bigger and better than they were to begin with, and I know that they'll still go on living for me, even after the story ends."

Joanne said, "I think I know how that feels. The characters you've made up are like friends you go back to. That's happened to me—I know."

"When you've read and believed what I've put in the stories, that's when they're truly alive," Martin said. "It's as if the equation's complete. I've done my best, and you've bought the book and done everything else. Between us we've brought something into existence that never existed before. It was a miracle, I once thought; a blessing, like making a baby. But there was something I'd overlooked, something that didn't come clear until I lost Josie."

"What was that?" Joanne was almost afraid to ask.

But in a sense, she knew the answer before Martin said:

"We gave life to the monsters as well."

A silence followed, and Joanne didn't know what to do with herself. She raised the tumbler to her lips, but she'd already drained it. She swallowed dryly while Martin brought her another. God, don't let it be true, she thought. But hadn't she invested as much imagination in demons as in heroes while reading? More, perhaps? Enough to bring them leaping and squirming off the page and into the world?

"It began with Josie," Martin told her. He was kneeling before the fire now, absently raking the ashes to let the flames through. "After she died, I never offered another manuscript to anyone. You'd be surprised by how much some would have been happy to pay, but I was starting to see the damage I'd done, not only to Josie but to others, readers like you. I couldn't stop writing—the stories wouldn't let me—but I could make damn sure I sent no more monsters out into the world."

Finished raking the fire, he took one of his books from the mantel above the hearth and began methodically to tear out the pages, a handful at a time. These he tore again and then again before lowering the fragments onto the flames. Joanne watched him, aghast; a too-large swallow of brandy made her screw up her face.

Martin continued, his eyes on Joanne as he tore out pages, halved them, burned them. "Still, there were monsters aplenty out there already, books on every shelf in every chain store. I couldn't do much about that—and at first, I doubted whether it mattered or not. I guessed it would be enough if I moved from the house I'd shared with Josie, began a new life, and tried to forget. If I could only do that—"

"But it happened again," Joanne said, sitting forward. "That's what you meant when you said this had happened before, isn't it?"

He nodded. "Not always, not in every town or city. But when I began to travel, I began to understand that just occasionally, here or there, there'd be someone so close to me, so emotionally charged, such a kindred spirit, that *things* would happen. Powers would be released. People would get hurt. You're not the first by any means." He turned the glowing ashes in the grate. "Still, there have been places where nothing has happened at all, places where I might have been able to live in peace. But always, at the back of my mind, there's been this need to move on, to be sure that everything's well in the next town."

"Here, for instance." Joanne leaned toward him, ignoring a soft thump elsewhere in the house. "So you came to Westbury and found me and—" Her gaze strayed to the window. "You saw quite quickly that something was badly wrong. Is that why you're buying up your books; to stop me from reading them?"

"Or anyone else like you."

"But it's too late for that, don't you think? I mean, there are copies of your books at home and in here, in my head. The damage is done."

Finished burning the first of the novels, Martin began on the second, an early edition of *Forbidden Worlds*. "The thing of it is I can't be too careful. What's happened between us could happen again. I have to—take precautions." Was there the faintest glimmer of a smile when he looked at her now? "That sounds almost dirty, doesn't it? But I don't care to run the risk of anyone else here in town adding to what we've already started."

"I'll give you that, but what about the demons we *have* let loose? What do we do about them?"

"I'm working on that," he said vaguely. A warmth billowed from the hearth as more pages burned. "What we have to ensure is that we give them no more strength than they already have. They've now reached the point where they're capable of anything—you know what became of Billy McGuire."

"Only too well."

"Believe me, he won't be the last unless—" But there he stopped, perhaps at a thought; perhaps at the scuttling of footsteps overhead.

"Martin, what's up there?" Joanne's fingers contracted around her glass. Almost immediately the noises stopped. The thought of what might be locked in behind those boarded-up windows made her cold. "Are some of them in the house?"

He seemed to need a deep breath before replying. "Yes, and God forbid they should go any farther. As long as they're here, it's all right. As long as these books are left unread—"

Joanne couldn't contain herself a minute longer. Rising from the chair, she took hold of Martin by the hand that grasped the ripped and torn novel. "You've been living here like this, knowing what's alive up there, keeping those creatures prisoner?"

"But wherever I go, there they'll be." Martin's face was aglow with yellow and orange firelight. She

172

could see the ten years of fear in his face. "If I could live some other way, believe me, I would."

Then she was hauling him to his feet, and the book was falling open and tattered to the hearth. "Martin, I want to see. I need to know what we're dealing with."

"I would've thought you'd seen enough already to know that." Still, he was rescuing the glass from her fingers and placing it on the mantel, taking her arm as he walked her from the living room. As they went upstairs, something thumped lightly inside the room at the top, and Martin said, "If you're positive you want to see, then I'll show you." Passing the door and its secret, he led her into the bathroom.

She could see right away that Martin had spent as little time as possible in here. Probably the thought of what was next door had rushed him in and out, never loitering. Towels were slapped wetly over the side of the tub, where a tap dripped at regular intervals. A mirror above the washbasin reflected only a blur through its coating of toothpaste and shaving cream. The linoleum on the floor was slippery with mildew and curled up wherever it neared the walls. An out-of-focus picture of the bathroom rushed at Joanne as Martin eased the mirror from the wall. In the center of the brown square patch he'd uncovered was a hole the size of a peanut drilled into the plaster.

"There you are," he said. "Now look for yourself."

It was a scene from *Psycho*, Joanne thought,

except that Norman Bates had peeped *into* the bathroom, not out of it. She steadied herself, one hand flat palmed against the dampness of the wall, her eye to the hole. At first she saw only darkness, but as her eyes adjusted to the murk, a number of shapes became visible, some moving, some still. She tensed as something brushed the nape of her neck, but it was only the warmth of Martin's breath. Then she moved closer to the viewing hole, until her eyelash was flicking the wall.

"Oh my God," she exclaimed, when she saw what had been growing in the room. "What *are* they?"

Some were asleep on the bare-boarded floor like heaps of rags. But others were darting this way and that across the room, through patterns of light formed by cracks in the boards on the windows. Now and again, one in particular thrust itself wildly against the wall or the door. As far as she could see, the creatures were almost human, though some had too many arms, and one was wafting a tail like a reptile's. All were milk-white pale, with stooping postures and hands that were only partly formed, the fingers divided by webbing. None had features. Wherever she looked, she saw blanks where faces ought to have been. She had seen one before, she knew it now; a figure like one of these had shot out in front of a car on the main street. No wonder Martin had been horrified to see that one had escaped. Unable to make herself go on looking, she twisted away, sliding in dampness, and Martin caught her before she could fall.

"Now you've seen everything," he said quietly.

"But Martin, they look so—"

"Incomplete?" He nodded, replacing the mirror over its hole. "That's exactly what they are. Ideas waiting to be finished. Stories, monsters, people, beasts that want to be made fully alive. And as soon as that happens, God help us. But I can't keep the ideas from coming; I can't stop myself thinking, can I?"

He was having to support her as he steered her from the bathroom. Behind them the sounds of the beasts continued, scratching, thumping.

"The ones making the noise are the worst," he said. "They are the stories I'm writing now, or thinking of writing—ideas that have crossed my mind and that I'm planning to do something with. The others, the crumpled and sleeping ones, are stories screwed into balls and thrown into the wastebasket. Even they would like to destroy me, for making them alive in the first place, then tossing them out. Do you see now why I can't afford to publish again? If these creatures were ever allowed to develop, if anyone should read . . ."

Though he stopped himself there, there was no need for him to go on. Joanne thought she knew what the rest would be. She had already learned firsthand what might happen, by skimming those pages of "Cereal Killer," by believing in ludicrous Honey Monster just long enough to wake him from print.

Step by slow step, Martin led her downstairs. In the swirling fog that was her head, Joanne sensed the pain fading. Either the tablets were doing that or the brandy. Probably the combination of the two was what had made her so sleepy. By rights she ought to be unable even to stand still for nerves, but when she slumped in the living room chair again, her eyelids felt heavy enough to close without her help.

"But what are we going to do with them?" she wondered. "You can't just leave them there, surely."

"That's something I'm working on," Martin said. For the second time he brought her the copy of *The Pied Piper*. "Here, read this. It shouldn't take long. I'd like to hear your opinion."

While she turned pages, he fixed dinner. An occasional clink of cutlery or a short rush of water in the kitchen reassured her. But she didn't seem able to focus on the words in the book, despite the large print. When she looked up, the room seemed soft at the edges. Still, the story was one of those unforgettable classics whose details she still remembered from childhood. Skipping the words, she followed the pictures instead, knowing she wouldn't be missing too much. In ten or fifteen minutes she had reached the last page, and the book had slipped from her hand.

Forgetting everything for a time, Joanne slept.

18

AND AWOKE WITH A START hours later. Outside, the light was beginning to fade. Martin stood watching her thoughtfully from his place by the window. A light rain was falling—and then she realized the beads of blue-gray on the glass were not water. She tried to sit upright, limb weary, her feet still tucked under her in a tight ball of cramp. As she stretched out her legs and attempted to stand, the room turned through ninety degrees and she was forced to sit down again.

Her senses still had to adjust to being awake. She seemed to think she'd been dreaming of rats, since her head still resounded with their rapid, small movements and high-pitched cries. It took her a little longer to be sure that the sounds were upstairs. Then she remembered.

"They become restless at night," Martin said. "Even in that room, they know when the light is going. And you know how much stronger the imagination becomes in the dark."

She tried to speak, but her mouth was too parched. Instead, she nodded.

"Do you feel better for the sleep?" Martin wondered.

"I will in a minute," she managed.

He brought her a bowl of chili with a glass of ice water and then sat with a notebook, tapping his teeth with a pencil while she ate. Even now, ideas were forcing themselves into the world through Martin. In the grate, the last of the embers died, smothered by a surfeit of book paper.

The food was more than welcome. Her stomach must have shrunk since the last time she had eaten, and Joanne quickly felt full to bursting. When she'd finished, Martin put down his notebook.

"Better?"

"Much." She nodded with enthusiasm. "Thank you for taking such good care of me."

"There'll be coffee to follow, if you'd like. And there's a phone in my study across the hall. If you need to use it—"

She decided she did. The sequence ended 007, as she'd originally thought, and she hoped that after tonight she'd have cause to call him again. Seated at his desk, she called Margaret, skipped details, asked

178

Margaret if she'd mind keeping the kids overnight. Then she tried Georgia, but Georgia was out, or at least not answering. As she hung up, something slapped the window to her left with the force of a hand.

It was more of the fungus, a lump as large as a splattered snowball. Perhaps it would be better if she and Martin left this place as soon as possible; but surely the stuff would find them wherever they went. It was part of the waking nightmare, like a dark and unwelcome thought that wouldn't be shrugged off. And in any case, Martin was unhurried. In the living room he was waiting for her with a large wad of typewritten paper.

"My latest manuscript," he announced. "My latest unpublished novel. It's the last thing I'm going to ask you to read."

She accepted the pages from him as if they were long-lost Scripture. "But you're supposed to be destroying your books to prevent them from being read."

"This is different," he said. "Go through it now and you'll understand why. Take as much time as you like."

Time, though, had a habit of escaping her as soon as a story took over. Days might pass by without her noticing. While Martin sat, smoking one cigarette after another, sometimes lighting one with the tip of the last, she worked her way through the manuscript.

179

Beyond the windows half covered with fungus, dusk became full dark.

Joanne read quickly and hungrily, knowing full well where the story was leading because she'd been through it and was still going through it, because she could now see herself at its center. Once or twice she looked up, shocked by a feeling of recognition so strong she could taste and touch the scenes he had written. But Martin said nothing, avoided her eyes, studied his burning-down cigarette. Then the novel ended abruptly, just at the point where she needed to know more. He had left it unfinished; he'd let her go all the way through and then cheated her of the punch line. She stared at him, astonished.

"It's my way of dealing with the problems I've caused," he said, his eyes on the slime rain at the darkened window. "It's the novel I should have done long ago. It's meant to work in the way my story of Josie did—as an exorcism, an attempt to beat my nightmares by writing them down. I thought that if I could tell my own story—the story of a man who makes monsters—I might put an end to the threat once and for all."

Joanne said, "Hold on, though. Let me get this straight. The man in the story, the author, the sort of Frankenstein figure—that's *you*. And the girl is me." She held the manuscript firmly in front of her chest to stifle the deep-seated shudder she felt in her bones. He had even included the supermarket scene; the scene with the pizza that would not die; the central idea of a storyteller being terrorized by what he'd created. Everything up to the point where she'd fallen asleep in the chair. "But you haven't an ending. There isn't even a hint of what will happen. How are you going to destroy what you've done if you haven't an ending for me to read?"

"The ending is where you come in," Martin said. "At least, I'm hoping it will be. Otherwise the manuscript is worthless; I'll have slaved at it for nothing." And now his intense dark eyes were watching her critically, while a lump of ash like a pencil stub dropped from the cigarette forgotten between his fingers. "Joanne, I need your help. It's the only way I can finish the tale. But before you say either yes or no, you deserve to know the risk that's involved."

"I think I can imagine the risk," she said.

"There's always the chance that one of us—possibly both of us—won't make it as far as the final chapter. I'm going to try something new; something that has every chance of failing, but there's no way I can do it alone." He paused for a second, perhaps trying to gauge how she felt from the look on her face. "Do you want to hear more?"

She did.

"I'm going to provide you with the ending," he said. "And you're going to live it."

181

At first she was taken aback by that; then it occurred to her that living out the story was precisely what she'd done from the start; unaware of what she was doing, she'd played out scenes like a character in one of his books, like the girl in the unfinished novel. Now, with the night seeming to dim the lights in the living room, she didn't have to consider whether or not to go through with it. When Martin had finished explaining what it was she had to do, she realized the decision had already been made for her.

19

MARTIN WALKED HER SLOWLY out to the car. While he started it up, she waited beside it in the soft wash of light from the cottage, her feet scuffing up gravel on the drive. When the engine was turning over, Martin stood holding the door.

"Are you sure you want to go through with this?"

She nodded, stiff-upper-lipped.

"And you've driven before?"

"I know the basics—how to go forward and stop. I'll be all right."

There was a lingering silence between them that felt to Joanne like a moment of decision. She didn't know what to say, and neither did Martin, and when he suddenly put his arms around her, she wanted to collapse and just lie there and not have to face the rest of the night alone. She buried her face in his chest, her tears dampening the fabric of his combat jacket until he eased her away, brushing her hair back from her face.

"Now's the time," he said quietly.

When he'd gone, she sat behind the wheel, the window wound down while she waited for the staccato *tap-tap* of his typewriter. A couple of minutes dragged past, and then it began, at first only an odd, tentative letter or two; then a string of them, a line, a paragraph. Joanne braced herself, releasing the handbrake, gripping the wheel.

He was writing about her in the car, sitting here, preparing to leave. He was tuning in to her feelings, to her painfully fast heart, to the fears and uncertainties spinning and weaving like dancers through her head; perhaps he was even waiting for her to move—which might explain why, for a moment, the tapping stopped.

Then it began again. She drove, away from the cottage, away from the sound of her future being written. Because the story had been unfinished when she'd read it, he'd explained the rest to her in detail. Now the VW was stop-starting along the drive as she tried to adjust to the pedals. In the headlights she saw nothing but blue-gray fungus, its smell as acute as mold. A man-sized lump of the stuff rose from one of the chairs on the lawn as the lights flitted past. Then, briefly, she lost sight of it. Had something moved, or was that the effect of the lights? The next thing she knew, the beast was halfway into the car through her open window, a man made of fungus.

Joanne screamed, forgetting whether she was supposed to be screaming or not. She'd made her first mistake by wandering away from the plot: Martin had told her to drive with the windows sealed up at all times, and now look what she'd done! In the blackness inside the car she smelled breath like spoiled food, recoiled from the touch of a hand that felt softer than dough as the thing tried to scramble inside.

All of a sudden the driveway was running out, and she knew what she had to do. Ducking left as the creature gasped a foulness of breath in her face, she hit the accelerator, at the same time pulling the wheel, swerving the car close enough to the gates to slam her unwanted passenger into the post. The whole car seemed to shiver with the impact, and then the only thing rushing inside was air. Not slowing, she reached and rolled the window all the way up.

Through the gateway, into the dip, across the stream that glittered like stars in the headlights. She didn't see the mud at the far bank, but felt it sucking the tires as she tried to force the VW up the slope to the woods. The thing to do now was remain calm. Give Martin's tale a chance to unfold. Avoid doing anything stupid, such as driving into a tree.

The one that was blocking her way, for instance.

The shock of seeing it where it shouldn't be caused

Joanne to falter, and at first she accelerated instead of braking. She knew she couldn't have driven off the path—she hadn't gone deep enough into the woodland for that—and besides, the tree stood alone, apart from the rest. It was only when she slowed, fumbling the headlights on to bright, that she saw it wasn't a tree at all. It was Billy's assassin, the shape with the knife in *Nightstalk*. Still clutching the blade, it had stepped out in front of her.

Joanne didn't wait for its next move. She sped straight toward it, sounding the horn, closing her eyes just long enough to avoid seeing its face in the light.

If the figure had been a tree, she would have been dead right there. She struck it head-on, but instead of the impact she'd expected to feel, there was only a rush of warm air and the sudden smell of rottenness, as if the figure had parted like a wave to make way for her. Ahead, the cart track was clear again. She followed the route the lights were showing her. Night creatures, insects, moths, a panicking form like a bird's, rapped the windshield and the glass at her shoulder.

She'd known she would have to face this and worse. Martin had told her everything. At the time it had been easy to agree and say yes in spite of the risk; but it was quite another thing to have to go through it. In the wipers that smeared insects across the windshield, in every minute tick of the engine, she could hear Martin's typewriter, could feel herself being written. God, her actions weren't even her own anymore. If she wanted to stop, go back, go home, would she be able to?

Cries she knew from the cemetery were rising on the night air as she followed the track between rape field and wheat field, her foot pressed flat to the floor. The cries were like those of Martin's ideas, the faceless ones in the locked room, except that these were louder and fuller, more highly developed. They were rushing toward her from the fields on both sides, drawn by the lights or the engine noise—or perhaps because Martin was guiding them as part of his plan.

She tried to swallow a cry that no one would hear. As long as she remembered that Martin was making this happen, there'd be no need to panic. She was safe as long as she kept to what he'd told her. Right now she was just a character he was inventing and describing, and she must be content with that; she wouldn't let him down as the others, the monsters, had done, breaking free to do as they pleased just as soon as he'd made them strong enough.

She brought the car onto the main road past the signpost and turned right toward town. In the blackness behind her she knew they were running onto the road from the fields to give chase. The thought made her shudder, but that was the whole point, wasn't it? She was *supposed* to draw them out. For a hundred yards or two or three hundred, she rode with one hand on the horn, letting them know she was here, calling them all to follow.

In the distance, the lights of the town looked softened. It was easy to imagine a fog lay ahead. But the way looked clear apart from the odd gasp of marsh mist, drifting in from the roadsides like dry ice in a horror film. The trees on the grassy shoulder seemed to lean sharply toward the car as she passed, but it was the dipping, swerving road throwing the VW toward them, then away. She was slowing for a dip in the road when something reared up out of the darkness, directly in front of her.

Her first impression was that another vehicle was racing straight at her, headlights full on. But the headlights were those of the VW, reflected in the eyes of something that had crawled from the shoulder, leaving a slime trail like a snail's.

It had come from the polluted local river, she guessed. Martin had made it crawl from the filthy depths. The stench was unmistakable, even with the windows shut tight. In the headlights she saw enough of it to be sure; a constantly shifting mass for a body that seemed to be made of oil and foaming industrial sludge; a multitude of arms or tentacles from which articles of waste were dropping—bottles, cans, the buckled wheel of a baby carriage. But the arms were just waves of slime, rising and slapping down to become one with the body again. She couldn't see legs, and perhaps it had none, but the speed with which it raced at the car took her completely off guard.

Joanne hit the brakes as the demon blotted out the windshield. She had already been slowing; otherwise her emergency stop might have thrown the thing clear. Behind her the cries from the ones who were chasing her came nearer and louder. But the windshield was blackness. There was no way she could drive on, seeing nothing.

She turned the wipers off and on again, flicked one switch after another until water jetted onto the glass. It shifted some of the muck, but not the face that had formed out of slime on the glass, a face with a hundred eyes staring in.

It was then she remembered the jack handle on the backseat where Martin had thrown it. Had he mentioned it when he'd told her how the story would end? It didn't matter. It didn't even seem to matter that it had been useless when he'd tried it on Billy McGuire. For the moment it was all she had. Grabbing the weapon two-handed, she swung it toward the window.

The impact threw her back in the seat and speared her shoulder with pain. The windshield disintegrated, the river beast fragmenting into a thousand pieces, a thousand eyes each to a separate shard of flying glass. In the headlights she saw some of the stuff slapping the road to form puddles. Whether

189

there was life in any of it she didn't care to wait and find out: She remembered all too well how Pizza-Face had multiplied, and besides, she had clear view of the road again.

Something thumped the VW from behind as she let out the clutch and took off. The car jogged forward, into the dip, and then she was racing uphill to the straightaway. The beasts of the fields had almost caught up. Another second wasted and they would have been clawing their way in through the space where the windshield had been.

Thank goodness for Martin, though. Even now, he was in control, guiding her through one fix after another. *Tap-tap, tap-tap.* Words begetting words, becoming pages, a chapter. Perhaps she would one day look back on all this and see what a high, what a roller-coaster ride it had been. That was to assume she'd live through it. Who was to say that something wouldn't go wrong? It had gone wrong before—after all, he hadn't been able to save Josie, had he?

But that was the kind of negative thinking that would ruin his plans. Martin was doing his best for her—everything she was going through had a positive purpose; don't ever let her forget it! Even the gas gauge that was signaling empty meant something.

Every horror story had its closed door, its secret, its car that ran out of fuel or refused to start. So Martin was resorting to clichés. Did it matter so much if it helped Joanne get where she needed to be?

At least, she thought, at least the VW wasn't about to break down outside some ramshackle empty old house with a history of insanity and murder: She doubted she'd have been able to cope with that. She pressed the accelerator, but the speedometer's needle was dropping steadily. She was midway between the first and second exits on the Middleton traffic circle when the car stopped completely.

She turned off the ignition, then waited a minute before turning it on again. The engine trembled and died. Joanne put her hand to the horn and held it there for a count of ten. No, there was no doubt about it; she'd reached the spot where Martin wanted her to get out.

It could have been worse. The town center couldn't be more than a half mile away, and at least there was light here, the welcome sight of street-lamps, the glowing front window of a large car showroom. Behind her there was only blackness, and beyond that the distant dusting of lights in South Horton. The cries that had followed her from the fields were somewhere in the void between, and still gaining.

The traffic circle was oddly clear of traffic. Could it really be so late? Joanne set off at a jog, crossing the broad roads to the median strip beyond the second exit. A few lights glowed on either side of the road—a nightclub, a pub with a huntsman and hounds on its sign, a grim-looking pool hall—but there were no gamblers ducking in and out of doorways, and no cars, not even the sound of engines in the center.

In the silence, her soft shoes slapped the ground more loudly than seemed believable. She had always thought they were noiseless, and now they were drawing attention to her. They were supposed to, though, she remembered. The more noise, the better. In fact she ought to be kicking cans along the gutter, throwing stones through windows to set off burglar alarms. She was doing exactly as Martin wanted, letting them hear her, letting them follow her through the streets. And now she could hear footfalls that weren't her own, and doors here and there sighing open.

Were they behind her or in front of her now? She hardly dared guess. If she thought too much about it, she'd never be able to go on. Her pulse was racing as fast as her legs could carry her, perhaps even as fast as Martin could hammer out words. For one brief moment she imagined him at his desk, thinking of her, describing the alley she was turning into, describing the crowds that were gathering after her.

She understood now why *The Pied Piper* meant so much to him. After all, it was the part he'd asked her to play in his story. The difference was she carried no pipe, and the monsters were being drawn by her fear, not by music.

At the far end of the alley was the bottom of the pedestrian mall. Almost without thinking, she'd found the shortcut to town. Where were the crowds, though? Where were the shouting matches and scuffles that erupted every night as the clubs closed?

Dodging between two concrete traffic posts, Joanne hurried into the dark between the shops. Even the mall was deserted. The only movements apart from her own were small: the flutterings of moths at a night light, the stirring of a thrown-away newspaper. There were none of the town's drunks bedding down in the doorways; no late-night freaks stepping forward from shadows to ask for a light. At another time this might have seemed a great relief, but tonight there were other demons to deal with, demons in greater number than in any of the books she had read. And worse, she realized as soon as she reached the top of the mall and the vacant main street beyond, the beasts weren't only behind her, giving chase. They were waiting at both ends of the street for her.

Joanne might have screamed if she'd had the breath. As she ran into the street, unable to stop her legs, she saw them emerging on either side of her, from doorways topped with purple neon, from side streets as dark as cellars, the whole teeming town of them. She had always hated the hustle and bustle of crowds; now she was going to have to contend with it. Because here they came from all walks of life, like mobs of soccer fans marching to battle, arms raised, voices chanting. Where had they kept themselves hidden all this time? How could one mind like Martin's conceive so many horrors?

She didn't dare count how many she'd helped bring to life, but perhaps the numbers weren't what mattered. What mattered was that Martin's plan was gradually coming together. He'd cleared the main street as if it were a stage or a film lot; he'd pushed back the scenery, called in the extras. Albeit briefly, she sensed him pausing over the Olivetti, taking a breath as he readied himself for the final onslaught. She imagined his fingers brushing the keys. For a beat or two, everything stopped—even her heart seemed to stop in her breast, even the cries of the monsters. And then she was running again.

There was nowhere to go but Arcadia. Straining against the heavy steel-rimmed doors, she slipped inside just seconds before the first of the beasts caught up with her. Its hand left a green-gray smear on the glass as she dodged away. Its one eye placed square in the center of its chest made her gasp, revolted. The escalators were directly ahead, but this late at night they were silent, unmoving. She clattered up to the second level while beneath her, downstairs, the doors were parted and screams rushed in. As she turned to the foot of the next escalator, a plate-glass window smashed somewhere to her right. One glance was enough to tell her that the mannequins were moving in Top Shop's display, some in bikinis, others in Sunday-best suits.

But who cared what the hell they were wearing? They all had one purpose, showroom dummies and slime beasts alike. It was a purpose that didn't bear thinking about. She should never have watched David's *Dawn of the Dead*: By letting those horrors into her mind, she couldn't have made this any easier for herself. When she looked again, she saw the first and quickest of the creatures, the ones that had legs, at the foot of the flight she had just taken.

Turning, she saw that she'd come as far as she could. There was one more level above this, but nothing up there apart from the rooftop parking lot. What had Martin intended her to do next? She was beginning to feel she was improvising, which could easily prove disastrous. She needed a minute to think, but her mind had blanked out, because something like a cross between a man and a centipede was scuttling up the escalator toward her.

She could either go up to the roof—in which case where did she go from there?—or try ducking inside the multiplex cinema. But suppose she was setting a trap for herself, as she had in the bathroom at home? What then? The only alternative was over the balcony and down, a two-flight drop to her death among the mirrors and plastic palm trees. Whichever, she hadn't the time to think it through.

Hoping she was doing as Martin had told her, she rushed to the theater entrance. The glass doors were fortunately unlocked. Shouldering them aside, she went in.

There was no one in the foyer, either at the box office or the confectionery counter. The curved walls displayed posters for forthcoming attractions, and there were hushed voices and music, muffled by one of the five studio doors that formed a broad semicircle around the foyer. Above each door was an electronically numbered sign that was meant to light up while a film was showing. At the moment only the first of the numbers was aglow. It took Joanne a couple of beats to fathom what could be showing inside. As a dripping webbed hand struck the foyer doors behind her, she jumped and hurried toward Studio One. The door closed quietly after her, shutting her in, shutting out screams.

Joanne came up eight carpeted steps, then down the gently sloping aisle toward the large bright screen with the red EXIT signs on either side of it. As she did, her silhouetted head broke the projectionist's beam, blotting out an actor who was rushing around his home, locking and bolting windows and doors. No one in the audience bothered to complain.

All the same, wouldn't it have been better to enter another studio, where the beasts might just overlook her? She must have chosen the most obvious place in the world. But it was too late now, and besides, this was exactly what Martin intended. He wanted her here, he wanted the monsters to follow her in. If she backed out now, his plan was in tatters.

From where she knelt cowering in the row, she couldn't quite tell whether the cries were nearer or farther away. Above her on the screen the man had entered the bathroom to shave. It was another scene she knew from somewhere—from the trailer she'd seen with Billy.

Jesus, had that really been only a week ago? She ought to have known that Martin would bring her back here, to the place where everything had started. Now, raising her head level with the tops of the seats, she peered through the gloom, surprised to find that almost all the seats were empty.

At least she hoped they were. But here and there, dark lumps like patches of shadow caused her to look twice. She was wondering whether some of the demons had already found their way inside when a burst of noise to her right made her turn.

It was the man in the movie, screaming because of the grayish slime that was slopping in through his bathroom taps and up through the washbasin's drain. Dropping his razor, the man reeled away, only as far as the tub itself, where more of the stuff was seeping through the showerhead. As he slithered across the bathroom floor, there was the sound of a door flying open.

Either the movie used Sensurround or something

had just entered Studio One. Joanne glanced frantically along the aisle, but couldn't be sure what she saw—the light level was dropping as the bathroom filled up with gray; it was as if the projector's beam were being slowly smothered. There was a traveling shot of the actor now, as he ran panicking from the bathroom and down the stairs; then a cut as he careered along his hallway and into the kitchen, where more of the grayish slime ran toward him in a wave. Wherever he went, whatever he did, there was always more: She was beginning to know how he felt. She had been exactly like that all along, evading one monster only to dodge into another's path. It was a feeling of helplessness that reached her again as a scream went up around the theater—a scream that might even have been her own—and a number of figures that had nothing to do with the film came rushing toward her out of the dark.

Joanne closed her eyes. That way she wouldn't have to see what was coming for her. There was a gushing noise—more Sensurround—and then the merest whiff of breath on her neck. If she opened her eyes now, she'd be staring into the face of something that would kill her with a look. Instead, she shrank farther into the blackness between the rows of seats, both hands covering her face.

"Joanne," a voice whispered.

They knew her name and had always known her name. But she was wise now; she wouldn't be lured out by a trick like that. In a minute it would be over: Until then all she needed to do was be patient while Martin tapped out the final scene.

Now it made sense. It was a scene as wild and as daring as anything he'd tried in his earlier books. *The Pied Piper* had long been a model he'd wanted to use, and the movie screen had given him a way of doing just that.

They might have been horrendous, the beasts he'd thought up, but they'd banded together like mindless sheep—indeed, like rats being led to a river. Except that there was no river here in the dark, only an ever-changing, ever-growing blob in a film that swallowed and digested whatever it touched. They'd believed they were acting of their own free will, when all the time Joanne had been drawing them here, to the rectangle of light and the deafening cries of the actor whose body was melting away.

"Joanne," the voice came again.

It was followed by a crash of furniture, a roar of music so loud it distorted her hearing, a long, tremulous cry from something neither animal nor human. Her hands were pressed so hard to her face that the nails were piercing her skin. She wouldn't look up— she wouldn't give the creatures that chance—but she badly wanted to know if everything was happening the way Martin had promised.

In her mind's eye she could see it all: the gray slime foaming into the theater from the the screen and through the twin loudspeakers on either side of it, forcing open both exit doors as the made-up monsters tried to escape. She imagined their shapes like shadows on the screen itself, breaking the beam, shapes that distorted and shrank while the slime from the movie consumed them. And their numbers were falling, the threat was diminishing. She could sense Martin Wisemann taking breaths—easy, extended breaths now—as the story came under control once again.

He was winning; she knew it. She had called his monsters to their final, wonderful death scene. She had played the part exactly as he'd asked her to. She raised herself up, opening her eyes, ready to wave her fist for victory at the screen; and then she saw the shapes looming over her, still trapped by the light, shapes that were reaching out their hands and whispering her name.

"Joanne, you'd better be coming with us," said Georgia.

20

IT WAS DARK OUTSIDE, though not as dark as when she'd dashed into Arcadia. Flanked by Georgia and Tim, each of whom held one of her arms, Joanne waited at the road's edge for a gap in the midnight traffic. When the way was clear, they crossed to the mall, sitting shoulder to shoulder on the first spare bench they could find, the others being occupied by napping drunks. Somewhere in the darkness between the shops, several girls with paint-peeling voices were bickering.

"Some film," Tim said, after a time.

"Yes." Joanne nodded. "I can't believe it's over."

"You'd better explain while everything's clear in your mind," Georgia said.

Joanne said, "Explain what?"

"Don't tell me you've forgotten already." Georgia

studied her, half frowning. "I'm talking about what happened back there. Why you came blundering in, throwing yourself about, hiding between the seats. Was somebody after you?"

"I—I thought so. I thought they—"

"*They?*"

Joanne gnawed her lip, afraid of saying more. How could she explain, when she couldn't be sure herself what had happened? She sat, unable to meet Georgia's stare, and instead watched her feet, which felt raw from running.

"Tim, would you bring us two coffees or something?" Georgia said, waving vaguely toward an all-night hot-dog cart on the main street below the mall. When he returned, the last bus from town was just departing. Joanne watched it go while sipping her drink, which burned her tongue. It didn't even have the compensation of taste.

"Would you like us to take you home now?" Georgia said. "Tim has his dad's car parked on Cyprus Street. If you'd prefer, we can talk about this in the morning. But I think we *should* talk."

Joanne shook her head. "I'm all right. Or I will be. I don't mind going over it now."

"You said *they*," Georgia reminded her. "Who did you mean by *they*?"

Joanne looked up sharply. "Did you see anyone—anyone at all besides me? Following me into the cinema?"

Neither Georgia nor Tim seemed to have. "Why?" Georgia asked.

"Because they were supposed to."

The others looked at her, dumbfounded.

Joanne said, "Before you went in, then, before the movie started. Did you notice any difference out here in the street? Did the town seem any quieter than usual?"

"It's Friday night," Tim said. "You know how it is when the weekend comes. No, I don't think it was especially different."

"Well, for me it was. When I arrived tonight, the streets were empty. Even the movie theater was empty. It was as if everything had become scenery in a story I was taking part in." She paused, embarrassed to see that they were listening with all seriousness, when really they should have been writing her off as drunk or delirious. "In fact, that's exactly what *was* happening! Georgia, do you remember what I told you about Billy McGuire, about the night he was murdered? Do you remember what happened at the lakeside, when Jason nearly drowned?"

"Yes." Georgia nodded. "Yes, I do, but what does any of that have to do with—"

"Martin," Joanne said, straightening. "Martin Wisemann is the one thing that ties this all together. Ever since last week, it's been as though I've been caught up in his stories, one right after another. All the bad things; all the worst things . . . I sound like I've flipped my lid, right? But I haven't. Martin would tell you. I haven't been the only one this has happened to—"

She was ranting, and losing them both in the process, she could tell. Their faces made her think for some reason of blank sheets of paper waiting to be filled. She sipped at the lousy coffee, if only to stop herself talking for a minute. Across the street a crowd of people—normal, two-legged, one-headed people; couples arm in arm—were leaving Arcadia.

"I *knew* he'd have something to do with it," Georgia was saying. "So you took my advice and went to see him. And now you're shaking—look at you! Is this what he's done to you?"

"No, it's . . ." Joanne had to think. Gradually, inexplicably, it was dawning on her that she was more afraid than ever. "I don't know. Something should have happened in there, in the theater. Something so incredible I couldn't begin to tell you. But it didn't happen, don't you see? I wasn't followed; they didn't come in after me. There's something important missing."

"You're not making sense, Jo," Georgia said quietly, and then to Tim, "I think we should get her home. Can't you see what he's done to her, that— that *monster*? When I see him, I'll give him a piece of my mind."

"Georgia, please," Joanne said, and then seemed to deflate, exhausted.

It was useless trying to defend him. How could she make anything she'd experienced tonight sound the least bit believable? Could she really blame them if they treated her stories as jokes? After all, she had been living out fictions, the wildest that even Martin could dream up. And for a moment the town *had* been deserted, it had *all* been the way she remembered. The monsters should have been finished, once and for all, swallowed into the film; and yet, at the death, at the crucial point, something had been radically altered; a detail had slipped out of place.

She couldn't believe it hadn't happened the way Martin had told her. If it had, then she'd have sensed it in her bones, would have known without doubt. If the demons had followed her into the multiplex, then what had become of them? If they hadn't, then where were they now? It didn't make sense, she couldn't make it make sense, not unless—

Unless what?

"Oh my God," she said then. Standing, she was hardly aware of the plastic coffee cup tipping from her hand to the ground. "Tim, can we go to him now, right this minute? Will you take me to Martin?"

"Yes, I suppose." He shrugged at Georgia. "Well, why not?"

205

"But *why*?" Georgia wanted to know. "Why is this suddenly so urgent? Jo, what's come over you?"

But Joanne was already striding away from the bench to the main street, lingering there at the roadside while she tried to think her way to Cyprus Street. "Jo, what is it?" she heard, and then recoiled from the touch of a hand on her shoulder. "Jo, we'll take you, but what's wrong? What's wrong?"

She swung around to face Georgia. As she did so, Georgia tottered backward a couple of steps, as if something in Joanne's gaze had startled her, as if she'd seen something there that was utterly new and terrible. Then she stood, waiting.

"He's changed something," Joanne said; and it was only now, speaking the words out loud, that the truth seemed to click deep within her and make sense, and a voice she had long tried to shut out began speaking. "He's changed the ending somehow," she said. "That's what he's done. He's changed the ending."

She wouldn't know what to expect until they arrived, but by the time they were driving, she thought she was beginning to understand what he'd done.

Why, though, when they were so close to completing his story? But then, it had never been his story; and the *Pied Piper* nonsense had never been his plan. It had only been his way of misdirecting her, sending her where he thought she'd be safe.

He'd used the monsters to guide her back to her friends, to Georgia and Tim, and all the time he'd been intending to call his creations home to himself. As Tim brought his father's Sierra bumping onto the main street, Joanne wound down the back window, thinking she was going to be sick. No, this wasn't the story of an author overcoming his deepest fears. It was the story of Frankenstein; the tale of a man destroyed by what he'd made.

At the main town traffic circle, the abandoned VW was still there and blocking traffic, proof of how real her journey had been. In the distance the sky was fringed with pale orange and lilac, a promise of better days still. After today, could they be any worse?

If there was anything to be grateful for, it was that Georgia and Tim asked no more questions. She wouldn't have been able to answer, anyway. At least Georgia knew her well enough to know she would need to explain, sooner or later. If only she'd been a little more like Georgia to begin with, content and self-confident, she mightn't have brought this disaster on herself or on Martin. She lolled in the back, her eyes heavy but sleepless, the brisk wind flourishing across her cheek. She was wondering whether she, too, would have to burn all his books as soon as this was over, when Georgia turned sideways in the passenger seat.

"Jo? Where did you say we were going?"

"Just along here, on the left."

"Where the sign is?" asked Tim.

"That's it. The turning for Westbury."

"Where the sky's turning red," added Georgia.

It was a harmless enough comment, but suddenly, before she knew quite why she was doing so, Joanne sat forward from the back, both hands tightly gripping the seat in front of her. "What was that you said?"

"The sky," Georgia told her. "Where the sunset is, past those trees in the distance. That's roughly where Westbury is, isn't it?" For a time there was silence and the soft, suspended motion of the car over uneven road while her own light dawned. "Jesus," Georgia sighed finally, turning through the dark toward Joanne. "That's the east, Jo, isn't it? And the sun set hours ago. It can't be the sunset. And it's too early for daybreak."

"I know what it is," Joanne said under her breath.

Tim began pushing the Sierra past the speed limit.

The emergency services were already on the scene when they arrived. A fire engine, an ambulance, and a mud-caked police car were parked, acutely angled, in front of the cottages, lights revolving. They were drawing water from the stream, and a cascading golden-yellow fountain stood highlighted against the night sky. Here and there, police wandered aimlessly, ushering neighbors in dressing gowns back to their beds. One officer came splashing through the stream, arms waving, as Tim brought the Sierra down the incline and into the mud. He was warning them off, but Joanne already had the rear door open before Tim had stopped, and neatly dodged clear of the policeman's lunge.

In spite of the dark, she found the stepping stones across the water as if by instinct. She didn't even consider where her feet were landing. Even before she was up the bank on the far side, she felt the heat from the cottage. Through the broad open gateway she could see how little was left of the place. Though the outer walls were still standing, the roof had collapsed, and the chimney with it, and the boarded-up windows on the upper floor were now like watchful open eyes, filled with flames.

Just inside the drive an ambulance attendant and a cop were muttering about vandals to a man from the local newspaper. If that was what they wanted to think, let them think it. She wasn't about to spoil their fantasies by telling the truth, not when the make-believe stuff was so much more credible.

"I'm sorry, miss, but you can't go any farther."

It was the cop from the stream, his hands outspread by way of apology. Behind him stood Georgia and Tim. Heat or tears or a combination of both had made the three of them appear unfocused, like poor reflections in Martin's bathroom mirror.

"I don't suppose there's any hope?" she said to the cop.

He shook his head gravely. "Half an hour ago there might have been. They're only just managing to force their way in. We know there were people inside; we saw them moving, and heard—" He didn't go on, aware perhaps that he wasn't helping. "Did you know them, miss? The residents?"

"One of them, yes."

"Perhaps we can ask you a question or two about that later on." He forced a smile that was supposed to console her. "Perhaps it would be better if you went back to the car now."

"I will in a minute." She turned to face the blaze again. From somewhere inside came the sound of shattering glass; the jetting water, like fire from heaven, shifted downward from the roof to the upstairs windows. It was a scene from the climax of a horror story. It occurred to her, as she stood there, that every weird tale had its closed door, its secret, its castle burned down to the ground with the villain within. She had read it or seen it a hundred times over, and now she was part of it; the story was stronger than she. The monsters were home, and Martin had sacrificed himself to make sure they stayed there.

And here was proof that his plan had worked after all: As the flames receded, the smoke above the rooftop seemed to rise and expand like a black umbrella, blotting out the sky. A cloud formed, and burst. There was the smell of burning foam on the wind and perhaps burning wood and a crash as someone, somewhere, took an axe to a door. Seconds later Joanne saw what was coming out of the sky, and realized with an ecstatic shock what Martin had done.

The air was alive with charred book paper. Wherever she turned, ideas floated down, burned up and forever finished with. A section of a page, the words lost to soot, wafted harmlessly down to her feet. She stooped to pick it up and it crumbled to dust at her touch. So this was Martin's last scene: a shame he wasn't here to enjoy it, since it was so much better than the one in the movie. Here were several ideas of his, burned to crisps, entangling themselves in her hair; and there went a handful of passing thoughts, carried high and away on a sudden gust of air. Would the thoughts cross anyone else's mind on their travels, she wondered? Would the winds carry them to others who might make use of them? She hoped not, for they were Martin's; and they were monsters. They had lived through him, and that was the way they should die.

She stood a moment longer, tasting the fumes that Martin's tales were making, closing her moistened eyes as the scent of scorching burned her nostrils. As she turned, she caught a passing black fragment and rubbed it into her palm. She wished there were something else she could take with her for a keepsake, but Martin wouldn't have wanted it that way. If he'd wanted anything of her, she thought as she followed Georgia toward the stream and the waiting car, it would have been that she forget him *and* his tales. They were told now, anyway. There was nothing more to be done with them.

21

GEORGIA CAME AROUND IN THE MORNING while Joanne was still clearing away the breakfast things. Helping herself to waffles and strawberry preserves, she sat at the kitchen table that Sarah and Jason had turned into a dump and listened while Joanne told her as much as she could about Martin.

At least Georgia listened with a look on her face that showed she wanted to believe. That helped more than she could guess. But in the broad light of day, the story sounded false even to Joanne, as if it had lost its power. The shadows had gone from the kitchen; the pizza crumbs under the table were just that, only crumbs; and in the open-doored basement, at the foot of the stairs, there was nothing except a smashed-up Hoover. She decided not to mention what had happened here, anyway. Enough was enough, and by the time she had finished talking, Georgia already looked shell-shocked.

For her own part, Joanne was beginning to feel empty and slightly depressed, perhaps as a novelist might feel at his journey's end, the work of months finally done. Plot lines had been woven, scenes slaved over and dumped; characters brought vividly to life, to become lovers and friends, only to be waved good-bye to forever. And Martin?

"They took a body out of that place this morning," Georgia said now. "It must have been his, don't you think? But they didn't find signs of the others you mentioned."

"Is that so surprising?" Joanne clattered pots in the sink. "They went back where they came from—they were never flesh and blood to begin with. Martin took them."

"That's one way of seeing it," Georgia said philosophically. "Kind of poetic, I suppose. Are you still going to do what you said, Jo? I mean getting rid of his books."

"I think it will be better that way. It's what he would have wanted." Not for the first time today, she wondered exactly what she would do with them, though. Selling them to secondhand dealers wouldn't help; not if there were others like her who might buy them. Martin would have wanted them removed and destroyed, no matter how many more copies were currently lining local shelves. There was danger between the covers, never let her forget that. As she washed out Sarah's mug with Sarah's name on the side and a layer of settled sugar in the base, she balked. Who would watch out for the demons now, in other towns, wherever there were people like her losing themselves in novels like Martin's? Rinsing the mug, she set it down with a thump on the drainer. Let them take care of their own monsters. She hadn't been the first and she wouldn't be the last, and they weren't her problem now. As you make your bed, so must you lie in it.

Turning from the sink, she saw Georgia getting ready to leave. "Well, whatever you decide to do, you must tell me," Georgia said firmly. "If it helps, I'll get rid of them for you." At the front door, she stopped and took Joanne's hands in her own. "I know you've been through a lot lately. I want you to know that I'm here—or there, wherever." She laughed. "You know what I mean. Will I see you tomorrow? It's the last day before we go back, re-member. The park, perhaps? On second thought, anywhere *but* the park. Will you call me when you know what you're doing?"

Joanne nodded. When she'd closed the door be-hind Georgia, she leaned back against it, wondering. Had Georgia believed anything she'd been told, or was she just humoring her? It would be nice to think she had one friend, one ally she could turn to at times like this, when she needed someone to share the fantastic with. But that was why she'd turned to books in the first place: In print, anything was possible, anything believable. For the first time, she could feel herself missing Martin Wisemann.

The telephone rang about half an hour later. It was David to say that Mary was still comatose, with no sign of change: He and her mother were on their way home and expected to arrive in two hours. That would give her time to clean up, get the place looking as it had when they'd left, vacuum cleaner excepted. She really should begin with the books, she thought, while they were still on her mind. Satisfied that Sarah and Jason were fine—they were currently shrieking and chasing each other around the overgrown back lawn—she went up to her room.

The bed was an unmade mess, a reminder of yet another sleepless night. On the table beside it was her open notebook, and on a clean page the heading: *Martin Wisemann—Thesis.* This she had underlined three times. Now, with her ballpoint, she put a fourth line through the subject itself. It was just like the old days again. Day after tomorrow she would beg another week's grace from Miss Rees, and Miss Rees would smile and shake her head sadly; and then she would write the project she should have written already. Whatever it might be.

The books seemed to fit less tightly on her shelf than she remembered—or had she mislaid one? For the moment, never mind. She began transferring

Martin's works to the bed, first the hardbacks, then the paperbacks. She would still need something to put them in. Resisting the temptation to glance at the pages, she began sorting through the pile to make sure they were all here. *Read me*, they seemed to be saying. *I'm only a story.*

Of course, she knew better than that now. She picked up *Into the Void* and smoothed her palm over its jacket design like a corkscrew's ever decreasing circles, and tutted at *Nightstalk*, with its unsubtle painting of a dripping cleaver and the blurb "He's thirsting for blood!" beneath the title. It was only now that she realized how prolific Martin had been—eight novels and three short story collections in six years. The only volume she couldn't immediately place was the one in which Sarah had scrawled in pencil. It ought to have been at her bedside, where she thought she had left it days ago. She could have been mistaken, though. She might have left it downstairs. Better to check right away, rather than leave it where others could find it. They mean business, those stories, she thought bitterly.

She was halfway along the landing and passing Sarah's open door when she sighted Martin again—or rather, his photograph, staring up from the cover of the book she was looking for. The copy of *Cold Comforts* lay facedown on Sarah's bed, along with a couple of her adventure-game paperbacks. When Joanne retrieved it, she found a ragged length of notepaper pressed between the pages for a bookmark. On her way to the landing, she opened the collection at the place that Sarah had marked; and as she did so she froze, as if a subzero draft had brushed her bones.

She slumped against the doorframe, weak-kneed. The day seemed to collapse away from her into silence, a silence she suddenly knew meant Sarah and Jason had stopped playing. Then their shrieks began again: It was perfectly all right, nothing she need worry about, it was only the shock of seeing that Sarah had been reading "Lover Come Back."

Or perhaps, more than that, it was the keen sense she had of the draft, of the air that seemed too cool by far for the bright summer sky, of the creak as a footfall drew her eyes to the stairs. The book fell from Joanne Towne's hand as she first caught sight of the shadow, moving just a fraction ahead of the figure itself. But worse, she thought, was the voice, soil filled and slow, dry as a coffin lid swaying open.

"I'm home, dear," said Billy McGuire.